AWKwaRd, *Victoria*

By:

Emme Burton

Copyright

Editor: Janine Savage, Write Divas Editing
Cover Design: © Sarah Hansen, Okay Creations.
Author Photograph: Dana Colcleasure
Formatting: Kristen Hope Mazzola

Dedication:

To anyone who has ever felt AWKwaRd.
You are anything but.

AWKwaRd Playlist:

Lips are Movin'	Meghan Trainor
Get Into The Groove	Madonna
I'm Not in Love	10cc
Alive and Kicking	Simple Minds
Slave To Love	Bryan Ferry
The One Thing	INXS
Big Decisions	My Morning Jacket
Head Over Heels	Tears for Fears
I Melt with You	Modern English
Take On	Me a-ha
PILLOWTALK	Zayn
Bizarre Love Triangle	New Order
Your Love Will Set You Free	Caribou
The Shoop Shoop Song	Betty Everett
You Belong To Me	Carly Simon
Lovesong	The Cure

Chapter 1

The Bet

"**D**iva, I'll bet you deep dish pizza, beer *and* sex."

Mariette Gallant, my fucking gorgeous blonde former prima ballerina boss, chuckles and says huskily, "I haven't had pizza and beer in so long I'd probably get off before you even touch me."

I circle around her desk, stand behind her and cup her shoulders, massaging them firmly with my fingers. Leaning down so I can breathe on her neck just behind her ear, I whisper, full of intention, "Oh no, the pizza and beer would just be foreplay. Trust me, I will *pas de deux* you so hard."

She shudders slightly but doesn't pull away. She turns her face toward my lips and exhales audibly. We're so close I could easily kiss her and set her on fire. I'm sure of it. So close I can practically guess what she's thinking. I'm aware

9

the effect my good looks and physique have on women. Mariette slides out from under my grasp, turns and sits her tight little ex-ballerina ass on the desk, using the chair between us as a barricade.

"B-bad idea," she stutters. She never stutters. Squaring her shoulders, she changes her tone to one of scolding. "Shouldn't date employees or students." Just what I thought she'd say.

"Who said anything about dating?"

She's talking about us, but the subliminal message is coming across loud and clear. I shouldn't date students? She knows it's my thing. Fuck! These bunheads are dying for me to crack them wide open. So is she. I can smell it on her. *Pas de fucking deux*.

She thinks she can put me off. She thinks I won't win. Dropping my head, I shake it and then laugh to myself before I lift it again and employ my best, guaranteed panty-dropping smile. "So, is it a bet?"

"Absolutely." Mariette scoots back on the desk, leans back on her palms and, spreading her legs, plants her red stilettoed feet on the chair.

Her white lace panties almost blind me. If I'm not mistaken, I can see wetness glistening on them.

She exhales and repeats the terms, "Three months. I bet you'll be crazy in love within three months. If you're not, these panties and what's beneath them are all yours."

I huff, and my balls contract in my dance belt. *Holy shit*, this cool blonde has me hot and bothered. I shouldn't be, but I am. And this bet is cinch. Fall in love? Me? With who? Women are my passion, my release, but not something to be taken seriously. It's not like there's anyone who's remotely close to "fall in love with" status in my catalog of conquests, anyway. I wouldn't even know what falling in love felt like.

Sex wasn't the reason I followed my older sister to dance class when I was ten, but hell if it isn't the best perk of being a man in a female-heavy career field.

Walking into that first ballet class was heaven with mirrors. All those beautiful girls reflected for my enjoyment. Fucking perfect. When I first started dancing, I was a short, chubby kid. The girls ignored me or treated me like a mascot or toy. Within four years, I was not so chubby. My shoulders and chest widened, my voice dropped, my arms became buff. And my dick? My dick was ready to go.

I run a finger up Mariette's leg from her ankle to her inner thigh just above her knee. Mariette just lets me.

"Fuck on it?" I tease.

Mariette slaps my chest. It just makes me want to take her now. "Maximilian, *that* is the prize. How about we shake on it instead?"

I remove my hand from her leg and offer it for her to shake, planning to pull myself between her legs.

Mariette draws her knees together.

Dammit!

She stands and shakes my hand. "It's on!"

I flip her hand over, bring it up to my lips and kiss her knuckles deeply. Her fingers flex. As I break the contact, I growl, "The pleasure will be all yours. Trust me. Thanks a million, Mariette."

Mariette laughs deeply again. "Maximilian Thanks-A-Million…, I'm sure you'll live up to your name."

I say nothing, but I'm thinking, "*Damn right.*"

Chapter 2

Three Weeks Later – Who's that girl?

"Call in the next one, Max."

Pushing open the dance studio door, I look down at the clipboard and call the next name. This must be a fucking joke.

"Awkward!"

Even as I shout the name, I'm thinking, *"Great! Judging by this girl's name, this should be a fucking treat!"*

"Victoria Awkward!"

A hand reaches down to pick up a dance bag among the sea of tightly bunned auditionees, and I assume it's Miss Awkward gathering her items. I turn to walk back into the studio, sure she's following me by the soft footsteps behind me. No need to make eye contact. With that name, this audition shouldn't last long. Still perusing the clipboard, I return to my seat at the skirted banquet table and whisper to my dick-stiffening boss and the owner of Gallant Ballet, Mariette, "Get ready for a treat. This one is actually *named* 'Awkward.' "

Mariette reaches over to run her perfectly manicured hand down my arm and then pats my hand. "Patience, Max."

I could get used to her hand on a few more places.

The sound of a dance bag hitting the floor and a deep, rich feminine voice enters my consciousness and wraps itself around my cock in seconds, making it twitch.

"Hello, I'm Victoria Awkward."

Mariette introduces herself and then me. Now I'm just praying she looks as good as she sounds.

"Yes, I know Ms. Gallant, Mr. Devereux. It's an honor to meet you, too."

I look up from my clipboard to see the *least* awkward thing I've ever seen in my life. A statuesque, slim strawberry blonde. Voice like a velvet hand job. If she moves as well as she looks and speaks, she's in. This one could give Mariette, the prize pussy I'm trying to catch, a run for her money. Who is this girl? Where did she come from? My dick had better settle down or it's gonna hit the underside of this table. Thank God there's a table skirt.

Thump-thump. Seriously? It's like my dick

thinks he's a Borscht Belt comedian.

"Knock, knock."

"Who's there?"

"My dick."

"My dick who?"

"My dick wants to come inside."

"Come inside where?"

"Your tight 'rooster loving' pussy."

I'm sure either my loud inner monologue with my crotch or my dick itself are going to get me in trouble. Better tame it with a firm push of my palm. I slide my hand under the table.

"What's that knocking sound?" Mariette asks.

Shit! I need to cover. "Sorry, I was wiggling my foot."

She shoots me a confused frown and whispers, "Nervous, Max?"

"No."

Mariette purses her lips and then continues with her questioning, "Not like you to 'wiggle.' "

Fuck! Why can't she just leave it alone?

She's right. I don't wiggle. What the hell is going on? I shrug it off. *Yeah, I wasn't "wiggling." My dick was just knocking to get out... or in.*

I usually show the prospective dancer the audition sequence, but since I'm sprung like a pup tent against my dance belt, I pawn off the chore off to my assistant, Rachel, by simply barking, "You." I lift my chin, indicating for her to demonstrate.

It takes no time at all for Miss Awkward to learn and master the choreography. Not "awkward" at all.

God dammit, she moves like a fucking dream. Those legs. That extension. I'd like to get her into an awkward position—on my lap with those goddamn legs wrapped around the back of the chair.

Mariette calls Miss Awkward up to the table. She is even more striking up close. Her eyes are huge. Blue-green. Pure. Guileless.

Mariette stares at her. A tight-lipped smile slowly appears. There is an uncomfortable tension between the two women. I can't tell what either is thinking. Miss Awkward doesn't appear nervous. Mariette gives me nothing. Does she like this girl or hate her? She generally doesn't call dancers to the table. If my cock wasn't playing human compass right now, I'd have given her a standing "O"—as in ovation. But the other kind of standing "O" sounds fucking awesome, too. *What's up with me?* I never respond to girls like this. Come on. I could do that entire waiting room by just smiling at them. What's so special about this chick?

Accusatory words rush thoughtlessly from my mouth. "Miss Awkward, you're seventeen…"—I look at the date on her audition form again, even though I already have committed it to memory—"eighteen in two days. Why are you just auditioning for us now?"

With a turn of her head, Miss Awkward briefly shifts her gaze from Mariette to me and then back again. She says evenly, "My mother felt I should wait."

"She may have cost you a promising career," I reply, a sneer in my voice.

"Now, Max." Mariette scolds me and finally responds to the girl, "Your mother sounds like a wise woman."

Not looking back at me, Miss Awkward replies, "To be honest, I don't always agree with her, but she's generally right. Generally."

Mariette stands and shakes Miss Awkward's hand across the table. "Welcome to Gallant Ballet."

I stand to do the same, carefully masking my straining junk with my clipboard. Our palms press firmly against each other, and there's a strong magnetic pull in the touch. Instead of removing my hand, I press it more firmly into hers for just a half second more. Instantly, I know where I want her hand to be. When I offer my congratulations, Miss Awkward's lips upturn, and I'm rewarded with a wide smile that parts her lips in surprise with the word "Oh!"

And again, instantly, I also know where I want those lips.

"Miss Awkward," Mariette interrupts, "I'd like to speak with you privately in my office. Max, please continue the auditions, I won't be but a moment."

Our newest ballerina moves liquidly over to her dance bag and picks it up along with a motorcycle helmet I hadn't noticed when she came in. Mariette stands and walks toward her office across the studio. Miss Awkward follows. As she does, she pulls a denim jacket on over her leotard and loops a set of retro-looking Panasonic headphones around her neck. She isn't like all the other cookie-cutter wannabe Pavlovas. No, this hot little dancer is something else. Something else altogether.

I continue to audition the remaining dancers, but am strangely distracted. *What's going on in Mariette's office?* If we like a dancer and offer her a place in the company, our financial manager, Theresa, usually deals with any contract and pay issues. Maybe she's just giving Miss Awkward a rundown on how things work at the studio. *But why the personal interest?*

After seeing Miss A's *grand jetés*, the rest of the auditionees pale in comparison. Still, I'm able to select one more girl from the bunch to fulfill the needed opening. She's a friend of Sylvie, my most recent bed buddy, and she'll do.

Just as I'm finished selecting the last dancer and gently letting the rest down with a "please don't hesitate to audition for us in the future," I notice the door to Mariette's office open. Miss Awkward steps out. Immediately, I'm struck that she is no longer wearing her pointe shoes but is now sporting somewhat worn high-top Converse—one white and one black. This girl *is* something different.

Mariette says something that causes Miss A to turn around and step toward her. In an unusual move, Mariette places a hand on our new ballerina's shoulder, smiles and says something more, and then a look that's something between a frown and displeasure washes over her face. She squeezes Awkward's shoulder. Miss A nods and then turns and leaves. I track her exit.

A snap of her fingers pulls my attention back to Mariette. I fucking hate when she does that. She follows it up with a motion for me to come into the office.

I don't particularly like being beckoned like a dog. I hold one finger up to indicate I need a moment and follow it up by screwing my face up into a silent growl. *Get the message, Mariette*? She can hold her goddamn horses. Mariette turns on her heel and strides back into her office.

Shit! I really want to talk to Awkward. I should go into Mariette's office, but fuck it! I blow Mariette off and hustle out of the studio and down the stairs in hopes of catching Miss A before she leaves. *What the fuck am I doing*? I don't run after chicks. I don't run after anything or anyone. Things, opportunities, women come to *me*. I don't even know if she'll still be around or how she got here, for that matter.

My internal questioning is quickly answered. As I push through the revolving door and step out onto the busy sidewalk of State Street, I look right and then left. My eyes catch a swath of light red hair splashing across the grayness of the day as she lets her hair loose, shakes it and then re-gathers it into a looser messy bun. She picks her helmet up from the seat of a motorcycle.

I call, "Miss Awkward!"

She drops the helmet to her side and turns toward me, pushing the black, too-large-for-her-face Ray-Ban sunglasses up onto her head. A look of genuine pleasure overtakes her, and once again I'm the recipient of her large grin and her adorable dimples. *Adorable? When the fuck do I call anything adorable?* I'm going to catch myself watching fucking kitten videos on YouTube if I keep up this sappy shit.

"Nice bike," I say as an opener. I know nothing about motorcycles, but it was all I could think of in the moment. It doesn't look new. The finish is matte black, and up close, it looks a bit worn and old fashioned.

"Yeah, isn't he?" She runs her slender fingers along the seat. "He's vintage. 1957 Harley. Belonged to my dad."

"He?"

"Uh-huh, I call him Mikhail, and I love him. I ride him everywhere. The fact that it pisses off my mother is just icing on the cake." She licks her red lips.

God, the things I could do with those lips! My own kind of "icing."

"Listen to me, yakking away. What can I do for you, Mr. Devereaux?" She removes the glasses from her head, places an earpiece between her teeth and bites it gently.

My mind swims with ideas. *What can't you do for me?*

I don't even know why I followed this girl out here.

"Uh, I just wanted to welcome you to Gallant." Jesus! I sound like the most pussy-whipped pussy in Pussytown. *Knock it off, Max.* In a sarcastic tone, I ask her, "Your name? Awkward? Really? That's a fucking unfortunate name for a ballerina. If that's what you consider yourself." I'm channeling my inner douche nozzle now. Being a complete tool has been very effective in attracting girls in the past for me. They think they can fix me. *Ha*! "You might want to consider changing it."

She doesn't flinch. "Never," she replies and lifts the helmet up and onto her head.

"Really?"

"I've had it for almost eighteen years. Someone would have to work really hard to convince me to change it."

She gets on the Harley, places her sunglasses over her sea-colored eyes, and pushes up the kickstand. She revs the throttle a few times, nods and says with a fucking perfect French accent, "*Adieu*, Monsieur Devereaux." Then she roars away from the curb.

"*Adieu*, Miss Awkward. Until Monday morning," I say to the exhaust of "Mikhail the Harley."

Mariette motions for me to sit when I get back to her office.

I let the door bang behind me. "Our new dancer is unusual. She rides a motorcycle. A vintage one, at that. Can you believe she rides that thing?"

Mariette smirks but doesn't seem surprised. "That's funny."

"She says it drives her mother nuts."

Mariette replies curtly, "Did she now?" Then she changes the subject, sort of.

"I see you selected Sylvie's friend, Alexis Tolliver, for our second vacancy. God, I hate that name. I swear every girl born around that time was named Alexis and every boy, Alexander. I'm surprised you're not named Alexander."

I chuckle, "It's my middle name."

"You see!"

"Anyway, run after *her*. Alexis. Leave the

Awkward girl alone."

"Why?"

"Don't you realize who she is, Max?"

"No."

"Awkward? As in the Awkwards of AWK Steel? Huge supporter of the arts in Chicago. One of Gallant Ballet's biggest contributors."

"So?"

"So, I know her family. Her grandparents. You've met them. The girl's mother isn't crazy about her dancing. Maximilian, I know how you like it when we get new dancers, but this one is out of bounds. Off. Limits. Do I make myself clear?

"Crystal, but Mariette, maybe she's *the one*? I could fall in love with her, and then you'd win the bet." I love to taunt Mariette.

"Max!"

"Don't worry. I won't let myself fall in love with her," I singsong. "I'm holding out for *you*." I point to Mariette's breasts.

"Tell me you won't make a move on her."

Like a grade schooler, I cross my fingers behind my back. "I won't."

"Don't give me lip service."

I stride toward Mariette. "Oh, I'd *love* to give you lip service."

Mariette stops me with her palm flattened against my chest. "Just don't."

I cover her hand with mine and push them south. Mariette doesn't stop me at first, but just as

23

we are inches away from the promised land, she yanks her hand away. I laugh and shake my head. So close.

"Absolutely. No problem," I say, lying through my fucking teeth.

I imagine having to break the "off-limits news" to my dick. "No *Awkward* sex for you, buddy." That's not gonna happen. Yeah, I can't get with Mariette's restriction. I'm going to have that girl. I'll just need to keep any "Awkward Fun Time" on the down low from Mariette.

The easiest way to make me want to do something is to tell me not to. Don't, won't, can't, shouldn't and basically anything that ends in *n't* gives me a *gigantic* challenge boner. Right now, I'm about to bust through my jeans. Mariette just issued an unwitting invitation to gobble up that little Awkward Strawberry Shortcake.

Chapter 3

Nighttime Choreography

I love Gallant Studios at night when it's quiet and I have the whole place to myself. The building is an old restored library that occupies the entire block of Washington between State and Michigan. Gallant Studios is on the top two floors. Tall walls of glass windows framed by sheer ivory curtains overlook Chicago and the lakeshore. You can catch the business of Michigan Avenue and tourists visiting the Art Institute or The Bean, which shows off distorted images of the impressive skyline.

Moonlight causes the warm brown dance floor to glow in the large, spare room. There's a grand piano in the corner. There are also two white leather sofas and a few wooden folding chairs that frequently occupy different positions in the space from day to day, depending on the angle Mariette wants to view the dancers, but that's all the furnishing. The room has twelve-foot ceilings. There are dance *barres* and mirrors on the three brick walls. One of the most captivating sights in my day is seeing all the dancers moving with the reflection of the Chicago skyscrapers and sky behind them.

It's unusual for me to spend a Friday or Saturday evening at work, but I just didn't feel like doing my usual weekend thing. Sylvie called to see if I wanted to hang out, which means hook up. I'm not in the mood. Something about that Awkward girl and the way she moved at her audition has haunted me all day.

I'm suddenly inspired to work on my secret project. The one I've been procrastinating with— been oddly stuck on, suffering choreographer's block. Victoria Awkward's dancing shook loose a few ideas, and I want to capture them. As a matter of fact, Little Miss Awkward might be perfect for the project. It's so private, so secret, I haven't even mentioned it to Mariette. I haven't mentioned it to a soul. I'm not ready to share.

I twist the rheostat on the light panel, which results in dim circular pools of light in symmetrical rows on the dance floor, and then I set up my laptop on the piano and boot it up. Navigating to my dance notation software, I review the last combination I worked on. The only combination, so far. This software is the perfect intersection of art meeting technology. I like knowing that my choreographic efforts can be captured just like a musical score. It also fires up my inner nerd boy.

Once I feel comfortable that I've memorized up to where I left off, I turn on some warm-up music for inspiration. Madonna's "Into the Groove."

When I'm working on a piece, I don't wear dance shoes or tights. I prefer to wear cutoff sweat pants rolled down on my hips. I never wear a shirt. That way I can see exactly what my muscles are doing and what shapes I'm able to achieve. Sometimes I strip all the way down to only my dance belt. Dancing with very few clothes on is a method employed by one of my favorite choreographers, Jack Cole. Most famously known as Marilyn Monroe's choreographer, he was trained in classical ballet, pioneered modern dance and merged it to form a commercial dance style that swept Broadway and influenced the likes of Bob Fosse. Don't get me wrong, I have a strong and abiding love for pure ballet, but I see no reason why other ideas can't be integrated.

And that's why I'm here. My unorthodox ballet. My baby. My secret project.

I'm well into the first sequence when a sight I never, ever expected to see tonight appears behind me in the mirror: Miss Awkward.

She's slack-jawed and gawking at me from the doorway. "Damn, you're beautiful," she finally says in a hoarse voice. She drops her dance bag with a loud thud.

I could say the same thing about her. She *is* beautiful in an unexpected, unpretentious, very un-ballerina way. Ripped jean shorts, flannel shirt, headphones around her neck, hair in a high pony and those Converse. Those damn mismatched black and white high-tops.

I turn in the spot where I stopped. "What did you say?" I heard her. I just want to hear her say it again.

"Uh, um… I guess I said, 'Damn, you're beautiful.' I didn't realize I said it out loud." Her face turns a fantastic shade of pink.

I don't say thank you or smile when I'd like to do both. I think she just tipped her hand. I think she might be attracted to me. And why the fuck not? I'm a catch.

I grab my white wifebeater off the floor and wipe the sweat from my chest and abs leisurely, trailing it down to just above my low waistband. I enjoy watching her trying not to watch me. "Why are you here?"

Miss Awkward twists the tail of her flannel shirt around her fingers and averts her gaze. "I… I'm nervous about Monday. Ms. Gallant told me I could come move around the space… the studio… to get more comfortable."

Mariette certainly is watching out for this girl. Probably something to do with the family association.

"Why are *you* here?" she asks. "It's Friday night. You don't seem like the type to work on a Friday night"

Wonder why she said that? "That's a pretty bold assumption, Miss Awkward. You don't know me."

"I… I'm sorry."

I'm being a total wanker. I'll give her a break. "My plans fell through. I'd usually make other ones, but I got inspired today and wanted to plot out my ideas while they were fresh." I leave out the part where I was inspired by her.

The music changes from the Madonna song to an oldie, "The Shoop Shoop Song."

"Is this what you're working on? A dance to the music of *Desperately Seeking Susan*?"

Wow! Even more surprising is this little piece of hipster hotness knows the movie these songs are from.

"Yeah, that's exactly what I'm working on. I'm choreographing a modern ballet version of *Desperately Seeking Susan*."

"I never would have thought of it for ballet."

"It's perfect for ballet. Just a gold mine. Farcical. Lots of comings and goings. Mistaken identities." *What the hell?* I just vomited up every emotion in the world about my project in five sentences. I delivered an impassioned elevator speech to a person I don't even know. I'm losing my edge.

Awkward suddenly becomes, well… awkward. She rubs a hand up and down her opposite arm and kicks a toe into the floor before abruptly saying, "Well, you're busy. I-I don't want to interrupt. I'll just… I'll go." She picks up her bag, throws it over her shoulder and turns to leave.

"No," I snap. *What am I saying?* I school my tone. "Stay." Okay, seriously, this girl has me under a spell or voodoo curse or some shit because I *never* want anyone around while I work, but for some reason, I want her here. "You can be my guinea pig." The words tumble out of me without benefit of thought.

She turns back and once again drops her bag on the floor like an announcement of her presence.

I stride over to her. "What are you listening to? Classical? Pop?"

Awkward stutters, "U-uh."

When I stand square in front of her mere inches away, I hear "Like a Virgin" coming through her headphones. I'm floored at the coincidence. "Madonna?" I ask. "I would have guessed Taylor Swift."

"No, I'm a fan of 80s music. I like vintage things."

"I'm from the 80s—1989. Am *I* vintage?"

"No." She blushes across her chest.

"Does that mean you don't like me?" I am *really* enjoying taunting her.

"No, not at all. I mean, I don't know you. I just seem to be attracted to things, people with a little... I don't know how to describe it really. Uhm... wear? No, that's not right. Maybe staying power? Patina? I'm not explaining this well at all."

"I think you've *nailed* it, Miss Awkward."

"Victoria."

"Victoria. Well, Victoria, like I said, I think you described it perfectly. It's exactly the reason I'm a fan of music and movies produced before the 90s. There's just something about them, you know? Like a time before everything was so instantaneous."

"Yes. Like right before the world lost its innocence."

Those words coming from that sweet young mouth make me even more intrigued. She's so angelic looking, but there's a wisdom about her. A knowing. I wonder if she is *like a virgin*.

"Exactly," I say, agreeing with her thoughts.

A wide smile lights up her face.

"I could use someone to help me with this. I've only ever seen myself go through the steps. Would you mind running through some of the combination?"

"Sure, Mr. Devereaux."

"You can call me Max, but only when we're alone. And, Victoria, when we're rehearsing with the company, I won't call you by your first name either. It's just the way it is."

"I understand."

She removes her headphones and drops them on top of her bag. I reach over and assist her with shedding her flannel shirt, which she has begun to shrug off. When my fingers graze the skin of her shoulder and arm, she shudders visibly.

So she's not as immune to me as she acted in the street. *Good*.

"Do you mind taking off your sneakers?"

"Should I put on my pointe shoes?"

"No, I like to choreograph barefoot in the beginning." I'd love to tell her to also take off the gray tank top she has on, but I don't want to scare her off and I don't think she's as "fast" as the other dancers I've hooked up with.

She leans against the piano and brings up one foot and then the other to remove her shoes. Goddamn, her body is so tight. I can make out every smooth curve under her tank top and shorts. Watching her move and stretch is giving me ideas about the dance *and* about how many positions we could get into off the dance floor.

I show her the first six, eight-count sequences. Victoria only needs to watch them three times and practice another three or four before she can execute them with a good deal of accuracy. After teaching her the first part of the dance, I move with her like a shadow, millimeters from her. We don't talk, only count out the combination. I occasionally correct her in a low, commanding voice, and she adjusts immediately. We're so close it almost feels like we're touching, but we're not, and it's fucking hot! I don't want to touch her yet. I just want this feeling to go on and on. Me directing her. Her complying. And all the while, that barely there, oh-so-close, tipping on the edge, anticipatory elemental pull.

And the way she smells—God! Edible.

Because it's nighttime, the windows act as another mirror, boxing us in with our own reflections, the flush of her exposed skin and the dilated pupils in her ocean-colored eyes. Victoria looks at me in that reflection, sensing everything I am. Suddenly, she breaks eye contact in the mirror and looks down at the large man's watch on her right wrist. Like everything else about her, even the hand on which she wears her watch shouts subtly of rebellion.

"Oh my God, it's almost midnight. I've got to go. My mother is a little protective. She won't be happy if I'm not home soon."

"Sort of like Cinderella, huh?"

Victoria sits on the floor and pulls on her shoes. "Yeah, but Cindy had way better footwear."

I chuckle. She really is charming. "Can I take you home?"

"No, I have Mikhail. And I'm just up at the Waldorf. I'm staying at my mom's."

"The Waldorf? Mariette lives there."

"Really?" She tilts her head with a small frown

33

on her face.

"Yeah." I'm surprised she didn't know that with her mother and Mariette being acquaintances and all.

As she gathers up her bag and headphones, she tells me, "I live at my family's home in Oak Brook most of the time. My grandparents' house. Mother splits time between the city and our house there. I'm just staying with her until I can get a place of my own." She looks at her watch again. "I really, really gotta go. Sorry to run off."

"That's okay" It's not. I want her to stay, but it's not like I can force her. I must actively remind myself this girl isn't yet eighteen. At least not until Sunday. "See you Monday, Miss Awkward. And happy birthday."

"You remembered." She smiles genuinely as she makes her way out of the studio. "Yes, see you Monday, Mr. Devereaux."

I think but don't say, "*I'm looking forward to it very much*."

Chapter 4

My Weekend of Diversions

This weekend has turned out to be supremely fucking boring. Every moment since dancing with Victoria has been disappointing.

I'm on edge. A sensation I'm not familiar or comfortable with. I haven't gotten any pussy in days. And worse, I haven't wanted to. I've had my phone in my hand to make the booty call to Sylvie several times, but I don't—or can't. Every time I'm about to do it, a vision of Awkward with her high-tops and her low voice wipes away the desire.

I've got to work off some of this unwelcome excess energy other than pacing around my apartment like a caged panther. Sometimes when I don't know what to do, I just need to hit something. Boxing. That's just what I need to do.

I head to the Celtic Gym. The place reminds me of the place I used to go in my old neighborhood in Dorchester, Massachusetts.

The truth of it is at twenty-five, I'm my own creation: Maximilian "Thanks-A-Million" Devereaux. Consummate player and professional dancer who gives no fucks. Actually I've given a ton of fucks. Every one of them resulted in a satisfied customer.

But before Gallant and before Mariette and her partner, Jerome Ward, discovered me. I was just Max Delaney or "Secret Ballerina," as my old man called me when he wasn't calling me Maxine, Princess, Maxipad or Twinkletoes.

See, I was born and raised in Dorchester, Massachusetts. Anyone who knows anything about Dorchester or DOT, as I call it, knows that Marky Mark Wahlberg and Whitey Bulger are from there, and it ain't exactly the rich part of Boston. And you know the urban legend that a long time ago when there were push-button phones, the phone company put up a billboard that read "Punch A Friend." They had to take it down after two days because too many of the residents were taking it seriously. Yeah, that's where I'm from. Columbia Point, to be exact. All four of my older sisters remember the old project. By the time I was born, they'd redeveloped the projects and renamed it Harbor Point, but the feeling was still there. The haves and the have-nots. I was born into the latter. I imagine it was sort of like Cabrini Green projects here in Chicago. But somebody had the good sense to tear *that* shit down. Where I lived was nicer, but still, it wasn't anything close to how I live now.

Whenever I think of living in DOT, my father's voice yelling at my mother rushes into my brain.

"Fucking ballerina dancin'? Are you fuckin' kiddin' me over here, Maeve? I'd rather he go to that fairy Irish dance place and hop up and down like a pogo stick than dance that pink tight shit."

"Frank, he's really good. There ain't that many good boy dancers."

"Right, 'cause every other father wouldn't fucking allow it."

To hide or mitigate my dancing, my folks sent me to boxing at Gallagher's, the oldest boxing gym in the Boston area and home of some major champions. This was old-school boxing.

My parents and Donnie, my boxing coach, agreed to spread the story that the dancing helped improve my footwork for boxing. It wasn't just a story. It was true. I didn't care as long as I got to dance. And the boxing kept me from getting my ass handed to me daily. You know, "Punch a Friend."

I'd dance from three to five after school and then go box for another two hours. It was brutal. After walking home, I'd eat something from the fridge and fall asleep by eight every night.

Boxing is not unlike ballet. You don't just go

in and start punching, just like you don't just fall right into a routine on the dance floor. My discipline in both is stringent.

Once I get to Celtic Gym, I spend time making sure I'm landing my punches accurately before hitting the speed bag and then the heavy. I finish off with sprints, landing as many punches as I can in thirty-second intervals, until my arms feel leaden. Clancy, one of the guys who works as a trainer, asks if I want to spar, and I do. It's obvious I've spent more time dancing and fucking than boxing in the past few months, because Clancy pounds the crap out of me. I'm grateful. I leave Celtic feeling exhausted and free from the tension that had plagued me. I barely think of Victoria and how I can't have her. That is, until I enter my apartment, alone.

"Goddammit!" I throw my gym bag in a corner and peel off my clothes as I make my way to the bathroom to shower. I'm down to my boxer briefs and about to turn on the water when there's a loud knock on my door.

Who the fuck is showing up uninvited early on Saturday night?

Irritated, I don't bother with putting on a shirt before yanking the door open.

"What do you wa—Sylvie?"

She's wearing a tiny black dress and her shiny, straight chestnut-colored hair brushes the tops of her breasts. I'm not completely unhappy to see her.

Sylvie leans against the doorjamb, tilts her head and asks bitchily, "What's with you? Canceling last night? Not making plans for tonight?"

"Quit bitching at me. I had something I had to work on!"

She steps forward, presses two fingers into my chest and pushes me backward into the living room. She eyes my crotch. "I've got something to work on, too."

Usually if Sylvie touches me or talks dirty, I'm hard as a rock, but nothing is happening down there. I'm so screwed. She leans forward and kisses me, but her touch is irritating. Her kisses are rote and nothing special. I don't respond.

"What's your problem?"

"Nothing. Just stuff on my mind." I can't get into this. "Look, I'm sweaty and gross. I need to take a shower."

"Let's see if we can get you a little sweatier before you clean up and take me out."

She presses her hand flat against my chest and continues to push until my calves hit the couch and I fall backward onto it. Then she pushes the tiny straps of her little black dress off her shoulders and lets it drop to the floor in an ink-like puddle. She is totally naked underneath and my dick twitches accordingly.

Thank the Lord. I thought it had stopped working for a second there. This Awkward chick is really getting to me. I'm never confused or conflicted about sex.

Sylvie drops in front of me and claws her hands up my thighs, her thumbs raking along the inner portion almost a little too aggressively. For a moment, I think of stopping her, but it feels too good. It's easy to rationalize letting Sylvie continue since the person I really want is unavailable to me. I pitch my head forward and back. Aaaah, I've trained Sylvie well. Under my tutelage, she's mastered all five ballet positions, *plus* position six—on her knees.

I lean forward slightly just as her lips find my cock. Running a hand down her back and the curve of her ass, I locate her already saturated pussy and rub her nub as she licks and sucks and powers onto my cock. Normally I'd be granite by now, but I'm just not.

My brain creates visions of Victoria Awkward pleasuring me, taking care of my cock. I close my eyes and picture Victoria's sweet cherry lips sucking me off. I imagine it's her in front of me. Her wet for me. Then I slip two fingers into Sylvie's hot pussy.

I can feel her contracting around my fingers. My dick is throbbing and loving every minute of my imagined Awkward blowjob. Knowing Awkward is eighteen tomorrow, I feel less creepy fantasizing of it being her. Pressure on the crest of my head stiffens me beyond belief. *Jesus! I'm gonna come soon!* It's all I can do to not scream out "Happy Birthday!" With Sylvie, at this point, I'd usually stop her, bend her over the arm of the couch and mercilessly fuck an orgasm from her until she's screaming into the cushion and yelling, "Thank you!" Hence, my nickname.

But this time, I don't. Tonight, when my balls squeeze and contract, I don't pull her off me. No, I grab the back of her head, pull her even further onto me and explode forcefully down her throat. Sylvie whimpers and gags a bit but swallows and keeps sucking as I continue pumping into her. I can't keep up the finger banging through all of this, so I stop pleasuring her, lean back on both palms on the couch and ride out the release. A massive cathartic groan leaves my body.

Sylvie removes her lips from me and sits backs on her heels, panting and wiping at her lips. "What the fuck, Max? How come you didn't wait until you were in me?"

I'll admit. It was a dick move. *Ha*! *Dick move*.

I rev up my best "I'm sorry" eyes and lie. "Sorry, pretty, you're just so good. I couldn't hold off."

Sylvie's a colossal narcissist, but I can't deny she's physically attractive. I also know I can get her off my back by complimenting her.

Sylvie flutters her eyelashes and pouts. "Well, what about me? I didn't finish."

"Get over here." I bend her over the couch as per usual, but since my dick is spent, I just tease

41

and rub and finger fuck her until she moans out the magic words.

"Thaaaaank yooooouuuu, Max."

Thank God I haven't lost it! Even though, for a fleeting moment, the "thank you" from Sylvie felt hollow and sad. The past twenty-four hours have had me doubting myself. I hate doubting myself.

I haven't really had a soft place to land my whole life. I just take refuge in the prettiest place or girl I can find. Sylvie worked well for that job tonight.

Victoria Awkward would be even better.

———

Sunday.

I'm more relaxed than I was yesterday morning. Boxing until you want to drop and then getting your dick sucked will do that. Well, I was—relaxed, that is—until Mariette texted me.

Mariette: Max, hope your weekend was good. Look who I ran into this weekend.

And then she posts a picture of Miss Awkward in the sexiest vintage silver metallic halter top known to mankind. It's so clingy I can see how tight and erect her nipples are. She's smiling. A huge grin. And has a plate with a piece of pink cake in her hand. Mariette is next to Victoria with her arm around her waist. I didn't know she knew the family *that* well.

Me: Where are you?

Mariette: Oak Brook. I'm spending time with Fleur in the 'burbs this weekend. Was encouraged to pop in on Miss Awkward's birthday party.

Fleur is Mariette's daughter. I've never met her. Mariette had her before I met her. I've seen pictures in Mariette's office. I think she's about nine years old. She lives with Mariette's folks outside of the city. Mariette's always talking about "better school district" or some shit. I don't ask too many questions. Kids aren't really my thing.

Mariette posts another picture of Victoria blowing out her candles. Goddammit! I can see her cleavage. It's perfect. Now, I'm thinking about the way she smelled. Like vanilla and almonds. Like cake. Delicious cake. I bet she tastes like cake.

This weekend started out great, and now I'm stuck in an obsessive thought spiral around Miss Victoria Awkward. Good thing I'm back to my routine tomorrow, even if she is there. It's *my* studio. *My* space. I can control things there.

Chapter 5

Monday Morning Rehearsal

Females outnumber males three to one at Gallant Ballet. I'm one of four straight male dancers in the principal company. That's a damn good ratio. I also happen to be the *premier danseur* and choreographer. The odds are stacked in my favor. *What does that make me?*

The only cock in the henhouse.

In addition to dancing and choreography, I split duties with Mariette as ballet master and mistress. Mariette works with the younger dancers. I'm in charge of the professional company. I run my rehearsals with the assistance of Rachel, a dancer who came to the company when I did eight years ago but has suffered many injuries. It's a shame. She is supremely talented both technically and artistically, which is exactly why she still has a job here as my assistant.

The professional company enters the main

studio after leaving their items in the anteroom. I don't allow them wear any shoes in here except their dance shoes. The fact that I was barefoot last night or Mariette can wear whatever the hell red-bottomed designer stilettos she likes are the exceptions. That I allowed Awkward in here with her high-tops on the other night says a lot. I'm already breaking my own rules for this girl.

Rachel starts the warm-up.

Ever since I heard her voice at the audition, I've been thinking about Victoria—all the time. I can't let on that I'm preoccupied. Not to her and certainly not to any of the other dancers. I don't have a plan to deflect, so when she lines up at one of the side mirrors to do her exercises at the *barre*, I act.

"Miss Awkward, you need to go to the inside *barre* with the other newer company members," I say a little harshly. I've been too solicitous. I can feel Sylvie's and some of the senior dancers' stares, so I turn to our other new dancer, Alexis, and say gently, "You, too, Miss Tolliver."

"Everyone, let's begin. *Pliés avec port de bras*."

Our accompanist starts, and the company works through *pliés* in every position.

In need of a ruse to watch Miss Awkward's firm ass and mile-long legs after snapping at her, I bark commands at her.

"Lift your chest!"

"Eyes on the head in front of you!"

"Focus, Miss Awkward!"

I throw in a couple commands at Alexis, the other newbie, but not as often and not as firmly.

"Center your hips, please, Miss Tolliver!"

"Check your turnout."

We switch up from the *barre* to *centre* practice, and I'm no less tuned in to Miss Awkward. I catch her giving a huge smile to one of the male dancers. The only reason it doesn't bother me is because I know he's as gay as the Fourth of July.

All I can concentrate on is her.

Shit!

While at *centre*, I come down on her about her posture, overextending her attitude in *derrière* and *pliés* that aren't deep enough. I expect a lot from my dancers. I can't go soft because this girl interests me. I should focus on Sylvie. She's the one who needs correction. Her posture and attitude are shit!

"Miss Awkward, move back here to the back. You need to watch the dancers who have been here longer." She really doesn't. She knows her *barre* and *centre* practice well. It's almost irritating how flawless her *tendus* and *bourrées* are.

With a trembling voice and lowered head, she softly acknowledges my request, "Yes, Mr. Devereaux." It's the first time she's spoken.

"And for God's sake, pick your head up. Get

your eyes off the floor."

"Yes, Mr. Devereaux."

Well, fuck. Is that all I'm going to hear from her? I want to talk to her, but there's no way I can do it here. Maybe at break.

We stop rehearsal at eleven. The dancers get two hours to eat and take care of personal errands before rehearsal starts up promptly at one o'clock. I'm about to approach Victoria, but I don't. I need to keep a little distance. Get a bit of perspective. I'm more thrown by her here than I thought I'd be.

Why is it when I'm agitated, my dick stiffens? Keeping myself calm and even while all I want to do is drag Victoria to the closest bathroom stall has been an all-morning struggle. Now she won't talk to me or look at me, and it angers me, which is making me harder. She must know it's all an act, right?

Fuck it! I have a boss to taunt and a bet to win. There's a way to get myself back on track and get my mind off Victoria, and it's only feet away. After slamming down a protein drink and popping a mint, I burst into Mariette's office.

She looks up from her desk, throws her pencil down and leans back, showcasing what's beneath her low-cut blouse. "Hello, Max. What's got you so worked up?"

"Just wondering if I made a mistake with the new dancer."

"Miss Tolliver?"

"No, Miss Awkward."

Mariette's eyebrows lift. She reaches for the pencil, rolls it around between the fingers of both hands and then taps the eraser on her lips. "Oh, really? How so?"

Pacing, I reply, "She's…" I search for the right word. Perfect? Delicious? Distracting? I'm going to have to lie. "Amateurish," I blurt out.

"Odd you'd say that, Max, because I was watching from the doorway for a while, and I thought she was doing well. Her *petits battements* were impressive. So quick—like the wings of a hummingbird. Not amateurish at all. Maybe even better than some of our other dancers."

Can't fool Mariette. "Like Sylvie?" I ask.

Mariette throws the pencil down again, comes around the desk, takes my hand and leads me to a chair. She turns it around and indicates for me to straddle it. She then starts massaging my shoulders.

Her breasts graze my back when she leans forward to answer my question. "Yes, exactly like Sylvie. Your slam piece is getting sloppy."

"Slam piece?" I laugh and then moan when she finds and rubs an especially knotted area.

"Is that not the right thing to call her?"

"Yes, that's an accurate description, but that's not your style."

Sylvie's hands move between my shoulder and neck. "I read the *Urban Dictionary*. I know lots of

48

things you wouldn't think were my style." Suddenly, she pushes her chest against my back, right up against me. Mariette rests her cheek between my shoulders blades and sinks her body onto mine. Her hands have traveled down to my lower back, where she massages momentarily, then slides them forward onto my thighs.

This has been the perfect distraction. "It doesn't matter. Sylvie's on her way out with me." Not too subtly, I change the subject. "You know it's been nearly four weeks since the bet."

"I know."

"Well, I don't know how you feel about it, Mariette, but I'm *very* encouraged."

"Are you now?"

I think I can feel her smile against my shoulder blades. Then she moves away. Massage time is over, I guess. That's cool. I'm calmer now than when I came in, and that's all I really needed.

"Max, it's almost time for rehearsal. I need to get freshened up. I'll see you out in the studio. Let me know when the company are all here."

Damn. Just when things were getting good.

Once the company reassembles in back of the main studio for afternoon rehearsal, I knock on Mariette's office door. She comes out, and everyone quiets. It's obvious she has an announcement.

"Hello, everyone. For those of you just starting, welcome. Today is the first day of rehearsal for our season starting in September. Over the next four months, we'll teach you part of the first show and then start casting. That will be done by July eighth. The theme for this year is "The Elusive Female." Our first ballet will be *La Sylphide*, followed by *The Sleeping Beauty, A Midsummer Night's Dream, a Balanchine Collection* and, finally, an unknown piece I hope to commission and premiere."

That's a coincidence—Mariette announcing a commissioned piece.

She continues, "If any of you, I mean any one of you, hear of anything, let me know. I'm looking for Gallant to do something new and different that incorporates my vision for the season."

I'm surprised that she announced something like that without telling me first.

As she's talking, my mind circles around her vision for the season. The Elusive Female. I begin to think about *Desperately Seeking Susan*. Who is more elusive than the character of Susan or, for that matter, Roberta, the confused housewife? *Should I tell her about it? Should I put it out there?* Not yet, but when the moment is right, I'm going to present the idea.

After rehearsing for hours, I finally grab a

moment with Victoria at the very end of rehearsal.

"Miss Awkward, I need to speak with you."

"Yes, Mr. Devereaux." She moves lithely over to where I'm standing away from the rest of the dancers.

I whisper close to her ear, "I'll be working on *Desperately* tonight if you'd care to come by."

Emotionless, she replies, "We'll see." She is strangely cool and composed for an eighteen-year-old. "I may need to work on my attitude."

Shit! I did harp on her about that.

Her expression remains blank. "Am I excused?"

"Yes, Victoria." I say her name quietly and directly to her, hoping to convey how much I want to be alone with her, careful that nobody else can hear.

"Thank you, Mr. Devereaux," she says, turns on her heel and stalks off.

She almost sounds pissed. Almost. *Why is she pissed*? I told her I wouldn't call her by her name. Did she expect special treatment because I danced with her one night?

I behave the same way every day—with Victoria. Every day, Monday through Thursday. It's working. None of the dancers in the company has any clue of my growing infatuation, but she has gotten chillier and chillier.

And every day at the end of rehearsal, I ask her, "Come dance with me tonight?"

51

Every day she says the same thing, "We'll see."

On Thursday, after I ask her again and she refuses, I go to the anteroom to pull her aside and ask her one more time. If she refuses me again then, *"Fuck it! What do I care?"* I think to myself. I can choreograph *Desperately* without her.

I'm just outside and can see into the room, but nobody detects my presence. It's then that I overhear Sylvie.

"What's his deal with you, Awkward?" Her tone is snotty and accusatory.

I see Victoria reply with a raise of an eyebrow. "I have no idea what you're talking about." She turns away and wipes at her eyes.

I say nothing. I'm essentially eavesdropping. *Goddammit, Sylvie! Leave her alone!* I have no "deal" with her. *What the fuck is she talking about?*

Sylvie directs her conversation to Alexis. "You haven't been here very long, but I'm telling you, Max is acting weird. With *her*, he's different. Angry."

I'm not angry. *Am I?*

"I've never seen him this tough on one person. Target them. It's out of character. He's acting like the Gordon Ramsay of ballet. He's not like that. He's more of a—I don't know—Simon Cowell."

Alexis giggles. "I don't know. I think it's hot when he corrects me. It's sort of nice to get his attention."

"No, Alexis. You see, with his dancers, Max babies them, coddles them, if he's banging them— like me. He dismisses them if they're used up or not talented. That's how you know it's over. He just leaves you alone. I found that out from Gia, his last one, after they were over and I got him. But he never barks at them like he does with Awkward."

Am I that transparent?

"Maybe he really doesn't think she's good."

Sylvie shakes her head and furrows her brow. There's venom when she says, "Maybe."

They're talking about her like she isn't even in the same room. *Bitches*! Victoria just continues to remove her pointe shoes and put on her jeans and Converse during the whole interchange. She doesn't say a word. I hear her dance bag scrape against the floor briefly as she picks it up to exit. I scurry around the corner so she won't see me hovering outside.

Sylvie and Alexis cackle.

I'm starting to get why Miss Awkward is so cool toward me.

I've taken this act too far.

Chapter 6

Thursday night

Thud!

She's here. The dropping of the bag on the floor announces her presence.

"Is it true?"

"Hello to you, too"

"Is. It. True?"

"What?"

"What Sylvie said today."

I know what's coming, but she doesn't know I was there listening, so I play dumb. "What did she say?"

"Give me a break. I know you were outside the room listening. You're not that slick."

"Oh." Busted.

"She said that you baby the dancers you're hooking up with and ignore them when you're done or if you think they're talentless."

"Are we hooking up?"

"No."

"Have we hooked up?"

"No."

God, she's frustrating. "Do I think you're talentless?"

"I don't know."

I tilt my head, shake it and frown.

"No?" she says, uncertainty in her voice.

"Then there's no reason for me to give you special treatment or blow you off."

"Then why are you being cruel to me?"

"Was I being cruel?" I'm not being cruel to her. I'm protecting her. Protecting myself. *Am I being cruel*? I guess I have been rather critical. Shit, I don't know what I'm doing anymore. I have no idea how to handle this situation.

Victoria nods slightly.

I lower my head, ashamed. "I didn't realize." I don't know how to explain. I can't tell her how much I think about her. How I want to be near her all the time and smell her and touch her. It's unnerving. "I think I may actually like you. I think I want to be friends. That's so fucking strange and unlike me. With a girl. I've never wanted to be friends with a dancer," I blurt out to her reflection in the mirror, finally saying exactly what's on my mind. Well, not exactly what I'm thinking—that would be pornographic—but what I think she'd like to hear.

Victoria tilts her head and wrinkles her brow. "Oh."

"You sound disappointed."

"No, I mean, well… No, I'm not disappointed you want to be friends. I'd like to be friends, too."

"But?" I probe hopefully.

"But I thought maybe…" Victoria looks over her shoulder to the window, her gaze far away. "Never mind. Let's just dance."

"Okay, then." I don't think she's going to say more. I walk over to the piano and turn on the music.

And we dance. And it's just what I want to be doing.

———————

After that, I change my tack completely during rehearsals. Now, I'm focused on making Sylvie squirm. Throwing her off. Off and under a bus.

Here's my new modus operandi:

Ignore Sylvie.

Baby Alexis.

Praise Victoria.

Then switch it around.

Ignore Alexis.

Bully Sylvie.

"Sylvie, your eyes are on the floor. People, where should your eyes *never,* ever be?"

The entire company answers in rehearsed monotone, "On the floor."

"Right. They should never be on the fucking floor." I get up in Sylvie's face. "Did you not learn that when you were five years old at Miss Prissy's Strip Mall School of Dance, Miss Marron?"

Sylvie says nothing, and I move on and praise some other random dancer. I'm having more fun than I should, tormenting her.

Victoria notices. She's smiling more and showing up every night to rehearse with me. I need to take advantage of this time to get to know her better. We don't have much time. It will soon be cut short when evening rehearsals commence.

Chapter 7

After Three Weeks of Rehearsing

Three weeks with no sex. Not with Sylvie. Not even my right hand is getting any action.

I'm unaccustomed to talking when rehearsing. Verbalizing commands and humming are about all I do. Victoria likes to chat. Dance and chat.

"How old are you?"

"Twenty-six. I came to Gallant when I was eighteen."

"How'd that happen?"

"Mariette and her dance partner, Jerome, saw me at a recital when I was seventeen and wanted me at Gallant. It was my shot. I just had to wait until I was eighteen. I panicked when Jerome died suddenly soon after that. I was scared the company would fold. You know who I'm talking about, right? The co-founder of the studio, Jerome

Ward?"

Victoria uncharacteristically digs her fingers into my shoulder as I lift her into a one-handed *presage*.

"Ow! Careful with your grip, please."

"Oh, sorry. Yeah, I've heard of Jerome Ward."

"It was a big loss to the ballet world when Jerome passed. I thought Gallant Ballet might not take off, but it did, and I feel like I helped Mariette get it to where it is now. I'm so thankful that Mariette didn't shutter the company."

Victoria mumbles hoarsely, "Me, too." I can't see her face in any of the mirrors, but it almost sounds like she's crying.

"Haven't been home since. I took off the second I turned eighteen. My caveman of a father's parting words were, 'Punk ass ungrateful fag. If you leave for that sissy fairy dancing job, don't come home.' So I did, and I haven't, and I won't."

"Go home?"

"Right."

"You've never been back?"

"No. But that's not my home. This is." I gesture to the studio space. "Until I make my own home."

We are in the middle of a sequence. Victoria is pressed against me with her front to my back and her cheek on my shoulder when she sighs. A long, heartfelt sigh that tells me she's sorry and she

59

understands without words. The segment ends with her character hugging mine and then leaving. She hugs me and launches into a series of *chaînés* and *pirouettes piquées* across the floor away from me. She is simply breathtaking, and I sigh to myself as I watch her.

Dancing with Victoria is a pleasure, but I'm losing my mind being so close to her while rehearsing every night. The only thing keeping me sane is going to the gym and pounding the bags since I'm not pounding anything else and don't even want to. I look a little rough these days with a split lip and an eyebrow in various stages of healing from being hit repeatedly during sparring. I already have a few scars from my time boxing in DOT. And some additional ones across my chin and neck where my old man thrashed me with a belt.

But what the fuck else am I gonna do? I'm not interested in any other woman but Victoria now. I'm even pissed at myself for giving into Sylvie the way I did. And now, I'm stuck in the friend zone. It's my own fault; I put myself there when I said let's be friends.

We almost have the whole three acts choreographed. The movements come together so easily and effortlessly. I'm sure it's because of my new muse. Just as we're getting to the ending and stop to talk through it, Victoria stares at me and then hits me with a question out of left field.

"Max, as a friend, I want to ask you to do something."

"What's that?"

"Stop boxing."

I stare at her incredulous. "That's not a question."

"Or at least stop sparring."

"Still not a question. Why?"

"I don't like seeing you hurt."

I mumble, "I'm already hurt."

Victoria frowns.

I guess I'm being vague. I should just come out with it.

Ironically, Victoria beats me to the punch. "Max, remember when you said you wanted to be friends?"

"Yes."

"I thought maybe... I thought maybe you might be... attracted... might want... me. I guess I was wrong." Victoria's breaks eye contact and looks at anywhere but in my direction.

"Aahhhh, but you're *not* wrong." Throwing my hands in the air, I turn in a circle and rake my fingers through my hair. "I'm just torn because while I *am* glad we're friends, I'm still a guy and you're fucking beautiful and unique and I've been told by my boss to keep my hands off."

"Ma... Mariette told you to stay away from me?"

"Yes, and to be honest, it only makes me want

you more."

Now Victoria throws her hands in the air. "God, I hate being told not to do something! Makes me want to do it just out of spite. Sort of like my mother and Mikhail."

She just sealed the deal. She's more like me than I realized, standing there verbalizing my thoughts.

I want her.

I walk right up to her, thrust my hands into her hair, pull her to me and kiss her roughly. That should give her an answer about how I feel. Vic runs her fingers over the three-day scruff on my jaw as she confidently kisses me back.

As I kiss her neck, I catch our reflection in the mirror. She has a small fleur-de-lis tattoo low on the back of her shoulder just at the edge of her leotard.

"Fleur-de-lis?"

"Yes?" She answers my question with a question, and it throws me.

I'm confused. "Huh?"

She shakes her head. "Silly me, I mean, 'What?' "

"You have a fleur-de-lis. On your back."

"Oh, that. Yeah. Hey, don't tell Mariette."

"I won't." *Seriously, why would Mariette care?* I ask myself the question and in the next beat recall why. "Afraid she'll say something to your Mom?"

"Yeah, something like that."

I turn her to face away from me and kiss behind her ear. "Is this okay?"

"Perfect."

I kiss all the way down to the tattoo and then back up to her other ear. Victoria reaches over her head and thrusts her fingers into my hair. I feel her skin pebble under my lips. She sighs heavily.

Our eyes meet in the reflection of the mirror as I run my hands up to cup her breasts and thrum her ever-hardening nipples with my thumbs.

"Confession. I've been boxing because after I dance, I'm a mess around you. Filled with tension and needing a release."

She watches my hands on her body, but doesn't touch me. "I th-think we can find a better way to release tension. One that doesn't hurt your pretty face." She finally reaches up and strokes the scars on my chin. I kiss the pad of flesh under her thumb.

I laugh. "*My* pretty face? Have you seen these scars?"

"Even your scars are beautiful. Max, if I promise to help you with your… tension, will you please stop boxing?"

"Are you sure?"

She spins in my arms and her taunt nipples rake across my chest. I pull her closer. Just having her in my arms relaxes me even while my dick begins to come to attention. Victoria's eyes widen as she notices my arousal.

"Yes, I'm sure. But Max, I may not know what to do. You may have to guide me, but I'm a pretty good learner."

"Yes, you are."

"And I don't think I could find a better teacher."

I have to ask her a question, and it could ruin everything. "Victoria, you know I've been with a lot of women?

"Yes."

"And it doesn't bother you?"

"I'd be lying if I said it didn't."

"Oh."

"And maybe I should be bothered more, but we've been spending a lot of time together and I don't see you giving anyone else attention. I know your schedule. I know how busy you are. You're spending all your time with me. So I may be a pretty little idiot, but I—I'm also a realist. I know the dangers, but somehow, I trust you. So I've decided to see what happens."

What do I say to that? Nobody's ever given me their trust. I have a sick feeling in my stomach, a completely unfamiliar feeling but oddly not unwelcome. She shouldn't have trusted me three weeks ago. I was still letting Sylvie service me then, but being around Awkward all the time— I've changed. At least a little bit, I think. But, I still have the bet with Mariette. Oh, hell.

The alarm on Victoria's cell phone goes off. She's set it to go off every night at eleven forty-five so she can get home by midnight. Tonight when it sounds, she groans and drops her head to my chest in frustration.

I lift her head with both hands and bring her gaze to mine. "I know you have to go, but before you do, one more lesson from the teacher." I run a thumb across her soft, full lips and then lower my head to allow my lips to take its place. The kiss is soft and lingering, and just as I believe it to be ending, my awkward girl surprises me and opens her lips ever so slightly to allow me to taste her sweet mouth and tongue fully. She steps back even as she kisses me more.

"Mmm." She breaks our kiss. "I don't want to go, but I have to."

"I understand." I turn her toward her dance bag and give her a little nudge. The last thing I want to do is have her mother get upset and refuse to let her out at night to rehearse, or worse, tell Mariette.

She slings her bag over her shoulder and blows me a kiss.

I catch it. "I'll see you tomorrow."

"Yes, tomorrow. No boxing tonight."

"Don't worry, Miss Awkward. I have no desire to box tonight."

Chapter 8

Getting Closer

I can't stop smiling… and I need to. It's going to be evident to everyone that something is up if I don't stop smiling and looking at Victoria, but I can't keep my eyes off her. Every single move of every single muscle is exquisite. She's good. Like, really, *really* good. I wouldn't be surprised if she snags a secondary part in one of the productions this season—she's that good. Of course, if things go the way I'd like, she'll be dancing the lead in *Desperately Seeking Susan*.

It's nearly time for me to introduce the idea of my ballet to Mariette. I just have the very end and a few more tweaks before it's in shape to pitch to her. I bet Victoria and I can wrap that up tonight.

"Max! Maximilian Devereaux!"

The calling of my name pulls me from my

reverie and brings me back to the here and now. Mariette stands in the doorway of the studio. "Rachel, can you take over for Max? I'd like to discuss something with him."

I nod to Rachel, tell the dancers to continue and make my way over to Mariette.

"Hey, what's up?"

"Come inside."

"Ooooh, my two favorite words... Are you sure?" I feel less of a need to flirt with Mariette than I usually do, but if I don't take advantage of that opening, she'll become suspicious.

Mariette ignores the comment. "I think it's time to cast the first two shows and start evening rehearsals."

"I was wondering when you'd say that. I figured we'd be starting soon. Some of the dancers have asked." Moving past Mariette into the office, my arm brushes across her breasts. Usually, I'd make a comment or linger, but I don't. I just it on the edge of Mariette's desk.

"I can't help but notice you've been behaving yourself, Max. Well, up until that 'come inside' comment you just made." Mariette runs her darkly lacquered fingertips up and down my arm as she walks by.

It doesn't affect me at all, which seems odd. "What?"

"Around me. With the dancers. You're not flirting as much. Not nearly as, hmm, what's the word? Incorrigible."

Weird. I guess I haven't been. I'm on the cusp of something with Miss Awkward *and* winning my bet with Mariette, but the notion of the latter seems to be less exhilarating than it had been.

I play it off. "Oh, that. Yeah, I'm playing the long game."

Mariette looks at me sideways and raises an eyebrow. "Wow, Max. You didn't even say that like a double entendre." She sits and lean backs in her chair.

"No, Mariette. I have my plan. It's working the way I want." I'm going to win this bet and I'm going to have Miss Awkward. I don't lose. Not at sex. Not ever.

"I'm intrigued."

I slowly walk the few steps over to Mariette, place a hand on either side of the chair, straddle her knees and lean over her body. Then I duck down, kiss her softly and slowly below her ear and growl, "You should be."

She shivers slightly before she pushes the chair back and away from me. She stands abruptly and clears her throat.

"We'll hold the auditions tomorrow afternoon and start rehearsals on Monday. That will give us the weekend to finalize all the preliminary plans." Flirting is over, it seems.

Okay, that means I must propose to Mariette that she consider my ballet for the commissioned piece because after this week, I'll have no time and no access to Miss Awkward to work on it for a while.

"Sure. Sounds good. I'll announce the casting for *Sleeping Beauty* and *La Sylphide* tomorrow and warn everyone about night rehearsals." Shit! I need to nail stuff down on my piece. And with Victoria. My time is winding down.

"Good, good. I hope you have some ideas of who you'd like for the roles. I don't want to spend forever casting."

Do I have ideas for the roles? I most certainly do.

Thud!

I love that sound. It means Victoria is here and all mine for a few hours. I don't turn around when I hear it. I just look at her reflection in the window in front of me. Coming toward me, taking off her flannel shirt, hopping out of her Converse and pitching them aside, shimmying out of her jean shorts and tossing off her tank top until she's standing behind me. She looks sweet and hot, grinning in her peach-colored bra and panties and long tube socks with red stripes at the top. Not her usual dancewear. It's quite a sight. I release a long groaning sigh only after I realize I've been holding my breath.

Turning around, I back myself into the curve of the grand piano just to admire her.

"Wow!"

Victoria smiles and bends to slowly roll off her socks. In doing so, she reveals the tops of her breasts. She looks up at me and smiles wickedly between attending to the first and second one. "I know how you like to dance barefoot."

I lick my lips. "Mmhmm."

Victoria slips down to the floor and takes the opening pose from the ballet just like Madonna's pose as Susan at the beginning of the movie: on her stomach with her feet in the air and her chin on her palms. Her breasts squeeze together, straining out of her bra.

My voice breaks as I say, "Th-that looks good, but I thought we'd work on the end."

"I don't want to."

"What?"

"Not after last night. Not after the way you kissed me. I don't want to spend hours dancing and then only get a few moments at the end of the night, right before midnight. Come down here."

"But—"

"Come down here, Max. I'll dance after you kiss me. After you touch me."

Who am I to refuse her request? I take three steps and then slide on my knees in front of her. My crotch lands right in her face and she giggles with glee.

I kneel back on my heels to get out of the position as Victoria crawls on her hands and knees toward me. Once she reaches her destination, she climbs my thighs until she's on her knees.

A buzzing, crackling energy flies back and forth in the minute space between our bodies. I break the perceived force field by snagging her around the waist with one arm and yanking her to me.

"Oof!" she says unexpectedly. "Yes, that's what I had in mind." Victoria is the seductress tonight and doing a fine job.

I run the fingers of my free hand over her eyebrows, nose and lips. Then I flip my hand over and brush it across her cheek before sliding it around her neck and grasping her nape firmly.

Victoria nods.

With that I pull her toward me and crush my lips to hers over and over. Victoria leans in and soon I'm sitting down with her straddling my now very happy and attentive dick. The heat from her core is causing a reaction from my body I'm sure she can feel.

"Mmm, I've wanted to kiss you all day, Max."

"Me, too."

Victoria pulls up the bottom of my T-shirt, only breaking our kiss to yank it over my head and then attacks my lips as if to make up for the seconds apart.

I move my kisses from her mouth to her cheek, then to the area under her ear and down her neck to her collarbone. Victoria arches into me, her breasts with rock hard nipples appear before my eyes. I move my lips down to kiss, nip and lick the upper part of her breasts.

"Uhh!" Victoria lets out a loud moan.

I gently bite each of her nipples over her bra, and she grinds and gyrates into my crotch. Suddenly, I'm the one moaning.

Too fast, this is going too fast. If I don't break away from her, I'll surely push her panties aside and fuck her in no time. I don't want this fast. I want it slow and deep. I can do hard and fast later. It's a good thing I'm so good at partnering because I'm able to slow things down as I spin her effortlessly so her back is to my front.

"But Max," she whines with disappointment.

"Don't worry, I got you," I tell her, and by only holding her by the nape of her neck, I lower her to the floor on her back. Our faces upside down from each other, I kiss her furiously as I slip my hand down her flat stomach and into her panties. I go just a bit further and find her clit, which is already slippery.

"Yes!" Victoria gasps into my mouth in her low, cock-arousing voice.

I rub her slowly and then with faster revolutions as her pelvis moves counter. We stop kissing and stare into each other's eyes, her gaze anchored to mine. The anticipation of watching her fall apart is glorious.

I slip my middle finger into her and keep the circles going on her clit with my thumb.

"Uh-huh, Uh-huh, Uh-huh!" she pants through slightly parted lips with each circle. Lips I'm praying are around my cock soon. Then she quiets and no sound escapes. I know she is about to cut loose.

"Well, well, well," a shrill voice interrupts our thrall.

Fucking Sylvie.

Embarrassed, Victoria whispers, "Oh, God, Sylvie. Max!" She scrambles away from my hand, and I quickly stand.

"So this"—Sylvie points at Victoria—"is why you're being such an asshole to me. Why you've stopped calling."

"Sylvie, listen." I have my hand up by my shoulders as if I'm being arrested. I have to convince her to keep her big mouth shut. I don't want her to scare Victoria away, and I certainly don't want her to tell Mariette about us.

"No, *you* listen, Maximilian—"

Victoria cowers behind the piano.

I march toward Sylvie, grab her upper arm and pull her toward the door to get her out of Victoria's sight and range of hearing. "Just get out of here, Sylvie, and forget what you saw."

"Why? Oh, I know. You're not supposed to be

banging her, are you? That's why you've been acting so weird and mean and secretive."

I don't say a word.

"I knew it! I knew something was up."

"Okay, Sylvie. You got me. Now. What. Do. You. Want?"

"I don't know. I just wanted to know why you were blowing me o—Wait! I do know! I want the lead."

"Are you crazy?"

"In *Sleeping Beauty*. I want to be Princess Aurora."

"So you're blackmailing me?"

"It appears I am."

"FUCK!" I yell and slam my hand into the doorjamb. "Fine. Done." I push her out the door. My only concern is Victoria and how she's taking this.

When I finally remove Sylvie from the studio and turn back around, Victoria has put her socks and tank top back on and is in the process of yanking her shorts up. She bends to snatch up her flannel shirt.

"Victoria, it's okay. She's gone. It's going to be fine."

"What was I thinking? Max, you'll get in trouble if we're found out, and my mother will pull me from Gallant in a heartbeat."

"They aren't going to find out. Not by Sylvie." I step forward and wrap my arms around her.

Victoria slides into my embrace. "She's not saying anything."

She nuzzles my chest. "I'm sorry our evening got ruined. We didn't even get a chance to finish." She looks back at the place on the floor where we were.

"No, *you* didn't get a chance to finish."

Victoria's deep laugh soothes my fears. "I meant the piece. *Desperately Seeking Susan*. But yes, me, too." At least she can maintain a sense of humor about being interrupted.

"I'll explain the end of the dance to you while you get your shoes on. Maybe you should go home early. It'll appease your mother. There are auditions tomorrow, after all."

Victoria agrees. As she pulls on and laces up her adorable, trademark black and whites, she approves of the ending I'm thinking of.

"I'm going to propose it to Mariette tomorrow."

I pull her up from the floor and into my arms.

"Good luck, Max. It's really good."

I kiss her sweet, sincere mouth. She hums. A rhythmic throaty hum, like a kitten purring.

What she doesn't know is that I'm also going to propose that she dance the lead.

Chapter 9

The Commission

I rocket into Mariette's office, plant my laptop on her desk and start up the slideshow. "I don't want you to say anything. Just listen."

"Max, the company will be here soon to audition." She shakes her head. "We don't have time."

"Mariette, calm down and watch. Besides, Rachel's going to get them warmed up." I wave my hand dismissively at the door behind me.

I worked all night on the PowerPoint after Victoria left. I meshed together photos and the music from the *Desperately Seeking Susan* soundtrack along with some video I took while rehearsing with Victoria.

Mariette watches intently, tapping her pen on her lips. When the slideshow is over she gets up and begins pacing behind her desk chair. She's pressing her lips together and bobbing her head up and down.

I can't stand her silence and begin to babble. "Mariette, I'd like to propose… No, I don't want to just propose… I want you to seriously consider *Desperately* for the commissioned piece for the company at the end of the season. Let me show you the notations." I search through the files on my laptop quickly.

Mariette comes over and puts her hand over mine. "There's no need, Max."

I keep searching. "No, I can find them. Don't dismiss the idea yet, please."

She squeezes my hand. "Max, stop."

I look up.

"There's no need because I don't need to see anymore. I'm intrigued."

"Really?"

"Yeah, really. It's different, edgy. People would expect that movie to be made into a musical, but a ballet? That's new. You know what? Before you show me the whole thing, like with some dancers *other than* Miss Awkward." There's an edge to her voice. "I want you to go to New York this weekend and show it to a few people. You know, workshop it a bit."

"What?"

Mariette moves back to her desk and picks up her smartphone. "Show it to some people I know at the Joffrey, American Ballet Theatre and New York City Ballet. Maybe even Madsen."

This is surreal. "Madsen. Like Peter Madsen? The artistic director of City Ballet, Peter Madsen, Peter Madsen?"

Mariette chuckles, putting her hand up to her mouth in a poor attempt to hide her amusement.

"Yes. That Peter Madsen. We're acquainted," Mariette says sarcastically and laughs at my expense, but I couldn't care less. "Now take your laptop and get out of here. Go rehearse the company. I'll set it all up."

I follow her direction. I'm about to exit when I have an idea. Spinning on my heel, I blurt out, "I want to take Miss Awkward with me."

Mariette cocks her head. "We'll see." The way she says it, her tone of voice, the coolness—it's so familiar.

———————

Auditions are generally a highlight for me in this job, but today, my attention is elsewhere. *Holy shit*! Mariette is seriously going to consider my composition. Thank God Rachel and Mariette are there to run the audition because I'm not on Earth right now. No, I'm orbiting the planet. Only two performances catch my attention. Victoria's, of course, which is gorgeous. Technically on point and graceful. The only way to describe it is *spunky*. I know how I would cast her. I wonder if Rachel and Mariette will agree.

The other audition of interest to me is Sylvie's. I warned her that she needs to be damn near perfect for me to even *suggest* her for the lead in *Beauty*. I can't back her for Aurora if she sucks. For her sake and mine, she must nail this.

Thank God she does. Sylvie will be a charming Aurora. I've been tough on her lately. The truth of it is Sylvie wouldn't be in this company if she wasn't talented, and, I finally have the balls to admit, I used her.

And she used me.

I hope she gets this shot. I honestly do, even if part of the reason is to save my own ass.

———————

After informing the company that the casting for *Beauty* and *La Sylphide* will be posted tomorrow morning, I wave Victoria over to me and move her away from the others in the studio, out of earshot.

"You look so happy. Why are you so happy? Auditions that good?" she asks.

"Auditions. Ha! I could barely contain myself during the auditions. I've been holding it in the entire time. Mariette is seriously considering *Desperately*. She's so serious she's sending me to New York to show it to a few people this weekend."

She whisper shouts, "Max! That's amazing." Victoria looks like she's going to hug me, so I step back. We still can't let on. We carry on our conversation in whispers and murmurs.

"And I told her I want to take you to help show it, and she said she'd think about it."

She points to herself. "Me?"

"Yes, you."

Victoria wiggles, bouncing up onto pointe and then back down. "I'm so happy for you. I want to jump up and down and hug you."

"Me, too"

"And kiss you."

It's taking everything in me not to scoop her up, spin her around and kiss her. "So will you go with me?" I whisper.

Victoria looks at the ground. "This is embarrassing. I feel like such a baby, but I need to ask my mother."

I step closer, but not so close that anyone would talk. "Don't be embarrassed. It's okay. I get it." Okay, I don't get it. Her mother is *really* overprotective. It is a little much to let your teenage daughter go out of town with a man you don't know, but this is business. Most eighteen-year-olds would rebel, but not Victoria. She's remarkably mature with the way she handles her mother, even if she rebels in other ways. Like motorcycles and the way she dresses.

80

She digs her phone from her bag. "So I'm going to go do that now." She waves the phone around and then points it at the door.

"Yeah. Go. Make the call." With that, she's out the door to call her mother.

———————

It isn't so much a thud as something sailing past my head and crashing into the wall next to the grand piano. It takes me a moment to identify the flying object. It's Victoria's dance bag. I'm equal parts glad it didn't hit me and truly amazed she has so much strength for so tiny a person.

"I'm so… fucking angry at my mother. She won't let me go." Victoria stands in the doorway to the studio, stock-still.

"Why not?"

"She's so overprotective, but she's not a helicopter parent. No, she's a stealth bomber parent." Accurate description, especially the stealth part. I've never seen her, not even a picture.

"That's it. Come on. Let's go see Mariette."

Victoria grabs her bag and checks the contents. She turns to the window and sighs. "It's no use."

The sun is shining, preventing me from seeing a reflection of her face. I step behind her and place a hand on her lower back. "Let's just see if Mariette can talk to her."

81

Victoria's eyes are wet, and she's shaking her head in defeat.

Taking her hand, I pull Victoria toward Mariette's office and enter without knocking.

Mariette is just finishing a phone call, but she looks up as she says good-bye and motions us in. "Max. Miss Awkward. Please come in."

Mariette's demeanor is formal, and Miss Awkward's posture has stiffened, her expression defiant.

"Mariette, we have a problem."

"What's that?"

"Miss Awkward's mother is refusing to let her go to New York."

Mariette turns her attention specifically to Victoria. "Yes, I'm aware. We've been debating that point." She points to her phone with a pencil. "Just got off the phone, as a matter of fact. I can see her side of this. She knows your reputation, Max."

I punch the air in front of me in frustration. "Dammit! That shouldn't factor, and you know it, Mariette. This is about the ballet, the season. It's business. Help me out here. I need Vic—I mean, Miss Awkward to show the piece."

"I know. And that's what made her change her mind."

Victoria's hands fly to her mouth, covering a squeal of joy I'm sure only dogs can hear. I can feel her shaking next to me. I thank Mariette profusely.

"Thank you, Ma—" Victoria whispers over her shoulder as I escort her out the door of Mariette's office, not letting her finish.

I murmur into her ear, "Hey, I'll see you tonight. Come back around nine, okay?" Victoria nods.

Once she's gone, I shut the door to Mariette's office and take a seat in front of her desk. "Thank you again, Mariette. You won't regret it."

"I better not. You're not falling in love with that girl, are you, Max?"

In love? Am I in love? How the hell would I know? I love dancing. Do I feel as much for Victoria as I do for my craft? That I'm even considering it amazes me. Maybe? I don't know. But I won't be sharing any of my musings with Mariette.

"No, she's just talented. Don't worry, I still intend to win the bet."

Mariette laughs. "Oh, Max… never one to back down from a challenge. I must say I'm impressed with your restraint. She's a lovely girl."

In my heart, I haven't been restrained at all, and I'm starting to care less and less about the bet. The only problem is I hate to lose at anything.

"She's more than that."

"Really."

Jesus, I'm giving out too much information. My feelings are showing. I don't do that. Time to bluff. "Yes, Mariette, she's a very talented performer."

Mariette's eyebrows rise like she knows something, but she says nothing and changes the subject.

"Okay, call Rachel in." Mariette rubs her hands together and turns the focus back to our task for the evening. "Let's talk casting. We'll start with *Sleeping Beauty*."

My mind is not on *Sleeping Beauty*. Unless it's the beauty I'll sleep with soon.

Chapter 10

The Way You Make Me Feel

Victoria is sprawled across the white leather couch in the dance studio, naked from the waist down. And I am happily facedown, making my way to her southernmost region. I kiss from her navel down the silky mound to find her slick and ready. I flatten my tongue against her clit and deliver firm pressure before lapping and sucking her rhythmically. God, she tastes like a sweet fresh baked sticky bun. I'm going to… Eat. Her. Up.

Victoria claws at my shoulders, back and hair as her abdomen and thighs contract.

"Aaarrrgh! Max, oh my God, Max! What? What's hap—" she screams as she comes all over my lips. I lick them greedily and then continue the steady pressure on her clit to roll her into two more waves of pleasure. The ones I didn't get to give her last night.

Victoria props up on her elbows, grinning widely. "What was that? Was that an… I just came, didn't I? That was real. That was an… a serious orgasm!"

I look up at her from my amazing vantage point between her legs. I tilt my head and then shake it. She's just so fucking adorable. "You've never had one before?"

"Yes," she confesses shyly. "But nothing like that—like, overwhelming—and not with a… a man."

She can't mean what I'm thinking. "With a woman?" I smirk.

Victoria's laugh is deep and centered. "No, not a woman. I've never had an orgasm with anybody. Man or woman." She waves the fingers on her right hand. "Only myself. I've never done any of this before." The same hand gestures in circles around her nakedness.

"What? Have someone go down on you?"

"Yes, I mean… No. I mean—"

I'm so astounded I sit up on my knees and stare down at my naughty, half-nude angel. "You. You've never been… fu—" Suddenly, I didn't want to finish the word. "You're a virgin?"

"Yeah, I'm a virgin, but not like a 'virginal' virgin. I know things. I've done things."

I'm agitated just wondering what *things*. "Really?"

"I've had plenty of fumbled make out sessions and near misses in the back of limousines with drunken, tuxedoed boys my grandparents arranged to take me out. I've come close, but to answer your question... No, I've never had sex, been... fucked."

I sense myself frowning. Seriously! No one has tried to deflower this beauty. Just the way she said the word *fuck* just now, with her bottom lip popping past her teeth, makes me want to throw her up against the wall.

"Idiots! Rule number one: Never drink so much you can't make your girl scream."

Victoria giggles and reaches down to stroke the hair by my ear. "Well, you don't have a problem with that, as you just demonstrated. I guess I just needed someone who could take control of the situation."

"Well, you know me. I'm all about control."

"As a dancer, I expect you would be."

"I've disciplined myself. That's all."

Victoria winks and licks her bottom lip. "Would you want to discipline me?

What the fuck is she saying? Is she asking what I think she is?

"I'm not into props, Miss Awkward. I'm all about the body. If I do what I'm supposedly a master of, I won't ever need to... discipline you. At least not with a paddle or a riding crop. I have a much more useful... instrument."

Victoria reaches up, grabs my T-shirt and pulls me down on top of her. When we're nose to nose, she declares, "I want you to make love to me, Max."

Surprised and frankly thrilled, I swallow repeatedly and finally find my voice. "For your first time, don't you want to be somewhere more private? Somewhere with a bed?" I can't believe I'm even saying the words. *When was the last time I took a girl to an actual bed?* The couch? Sure. Up against a wall? Fuck yeah! But a bed?

"No. No bed sex."

This girl is too good to be true. Bed sex is intimate. And yet with her, I'm considering it.

"Are you for real? Most girls expect to be swept off their feet to a big, pink cloud of a bed the first time." When did I become so sensitive or concerned with a girl's feelings? Jeez, this friendship—friends with benefits—whatever it is, is changing me.

Victoria sits up more and continues to stroke my hair, which I don't mind at all. "You'll find I'm not like most girls."

"I'm beginning to grasp that. Victoria, sex isn't always so great the first time. For girls. At least that's what I've heard."

While I've been talking to her, I've been intermittently leaving kisses on her bare shoulders. Victoria takes one of my hands and slides it to her breast. Then she reaches down and cups my dick.

88

My dick, which just happens to have jumped to attention during all this pussy eating and fuck talk.

"Just take me. I'm fucking begging."

I told Mariette I wouldn't go after Miss Awkward, but it seems things have worked to my advantage. I'm not going after her. *She* is coming after *me*. *She* said *take me*. Victoria strokes the head of my dick rapidly. That, along with the swearing and begging, has brought Max Junior to life.

"I can't think of anything I'd like to do more. Where would you like to do it?"

"Here."

I think of all the girls before her I've had on a couch. Even this very one. "Oh no, no, if you're not going to let me take you to bed, we aren't doing this on a couch. No." I back off the couch and pull her to her feet, which causes her to lose touch with my cock. I'm immediately sorry I did that, but I'm going to do everything I can to make this memorable. I pull her over to the piano.

"Here?"

"No, I can just see us breaking it. How could we explain that?"

I walk her over to the window and press her naked backside to the glass. "Here?"

"It's a possibility. We'll see."

"Miss Awkward, I'm running out of ideas."

"So quickly, Mr. Devereaux?"

I'm about to suggest at the *barre* when

Victoria cuts me off. I store away the idea for later.

"I know." Victoria's eyes widen with mischief. "Mariette's office. On that big desk of hers."

Our eyes meet. We both nod once and then run to Mariette's door. God, I hope she hasn't locked it.

Success! It's open. The lights are dim. Mariette has left her music on. Weirdly enough, it's Bryan Ferry's "Slave to Love." 80s music. Sexy. Perfect. The desk is completely cleared off. I imagined I'd be doing this with Mariette in here sometime soon. Now I can only think of how close I am to having Victoria.

We step through the door, and I reach down and take her hand. Bringing it up to my lips, I kiss the back of it deeply, then flip it over and nip each of her fingertips. Victoria watches. Little sighs and purrs escape her. Each one stiffens my dick further.

She finally turns to me, lifting her thigh ever so slightly to graze it against mine.

She is naked except for her sports bra, and I only have on my loose gray sweat shorts. I immediately reach between her breasts to undo the clasp. As I free her breasts and help her with removing it, I glide the backs of both hands over her warm, pink mounds. God, her skin is soft. My pinkies catch on her hard-pebbled nipples, and she moans.

When I've finished undressing her, Victoria

eagerly slides her hands between my shorts and my hips. She runs them down my ass, effectively pushing my shorts down. At least in the back. The front snags on my throbbing erection, and I assist her to get them off completely. As I do, she looks down between us.

"Oh my."

Her breath reaches my dick, and I'm no longer willing to engage in slow motion activity. I pull her to me, letting her feel the thickness of my cock against her abdomen. Not good enough. Not close enough. I grab the back of her knee and pull it up and around my hip. I can now feel her already slick and primed core sliding along my shaft.

Victoria thrusts her hands into my hair and pulls my face forcefully down to hers. There's a moment of pain followed by a wash of pleasure when our lips crash together. I can't wait to fuck her. All the things I want to do to her with my dick I do to her lips and tongue with my mouth. I dive in and lick and suck and kiss her until I feel her heart beating in her lips.

Victoria's hands are everywhere: in my hair, splayed out on my chest and finally down my side to grab my ass, pulling me closer.

I snatch her other leg, pull it up to my other hip and pick her up. Now I have her fully against me, our parts pressed together. I walk her over to Mariette's desk and seat her just on the edge.

"Oh, that's cold!" Victoria exclaims as she

lands. Her body leaves me as she props herself up on the desk, her arms behind her, palms down.

I slide my hand down to her clit and rotate my thumb right on it.

Victoria's head pitches back. "Aarrggh," she says from deep in her chest. She's wet from her previous orgasms.

When I thrust a finger into her, she groans again and her walls contract. Oh, she's ready.

"This could hurt, okay."

"I know, but…" Victoria reaches up, grabs the back of my neck, pulls our foreheads together and says, "Please, I want you so much. Please."

"I want you, too. I l—" I almost said I love you. *What the fuck*? Victoria reaches down and grabs my cock, immediately distracts me from verbalizing my thought, and I catch myself in time, saying, "I want to be in you so bad but—"

"But what?"

I look over my shoulder around the room. "The condom is in my shorts and my shorts are…" I twist in place and look around the room.

Victoria finishes the sentence. "Right behind you on the chair. Reach back."

I arch back to snag my shorts with one finger. Victoria never lets go of my cock. As a matter of fact, she runs her thumb up and down the shaft. Being a dancer and being so flexible has its advantages.

I'm hanging on, but I can't wait much longer.

After ripping open the condom package with my teeth, I try to hand it to her. Victoria shakes her head no.

"What?" *Oh, my God, what is she saying? Are we stopping?*

She keeps shaking her head and refusing to take the condom. "This is no time for a lesson. You do it. Next time."

She's a smart one. I roll the condom on, bring Victoria's legs up around my hips, line my dick up with her soaking core and push in hard. There's a fair bit of resistance, and then it's as if my dick has broken through a wall and entered a rushing, pounding waterfall. Victoria lets out a small yelp.

I moan into her ear, "You okay?"

"Uh-huh. I'm okay. You?"

She feels perfect. Tight and warm and wet. I get the overwhelming sense I've finally found the place I belong. Like I've finally found my soft place to land.

"It's heaven. You're heaven." I stay still for a bit until she's used to me inside her, and then I start to move, slowly rocking into her until I'm fully seated.

"Max, it's okay. Go faster. Because I need to move, and I need you to move."

I couldn't have dreamed up a more perfect sex partner.

I rock and thrust and circle a few times. She's so tight I know I won't be able to hold on. Victoria suddenly lurches forward, grabs my back and then her pussy contracts repeatedly around my dick. I let loose with a thunderous groan of her name, "VIC-TOR-I—" I don't quite finish her name, and it sounds like I've said "Victory" instead of "Victoria."

Victoria clings to me, panting into my chest and shoulder. I exhale repeatedly, feeling a little dizzy.

"Whoa!" When we separate a bit, I take her chin in my hands and lift her face up to look at her. She's flushed, her hair is a mess and she has an incredibly satisfied smile on her face.

"Victory, huh?" Victoria teases with a wink.

I laugh. "I was trying to say your name, but it did feel like victory."

"I'm glad."

"You're all right? You feel okay?"

"I feel great. I can't believe I can make you feel that way."

"You were brilliant. Did you come?"

"Yeah. A little."

"That's really unusual for a first time."

"Well, it wasn't my first time." She points toward the door and the couch. "Remember? The couch? You know, like, just a little while ago. Guess we'll have to practice to get to that level during actual sex."

"Oh yeah, you bet we will."

Victoria tilts her head and smirks. "Or you

could just keep going down on me on the couch."

"You've certainly figured out what you like, haven't you?"

"Mmhmm."

I grunt a bit as I pull out of her. I hate to leave. "Whatever you like, Miss Awkward. I'm good either way." I grab the top of the condom, remove it and then tie it off.

Victoria watches as I wrap it up in a tissue. "I guess we shouldn't leave that in Ms. Gallant's office?"

"No, that would be pretty bad form. Not that screwing on her desk isn't."

Victoria slaps my chest. I yank a few more tissues from the box on Mariette's desk, wipe myself and then kneel before her to clean her up. She purrs through the entire thing.

"You may be sore tomorrow."

"I think it will be a good kind of sore." She gets off the desk and searches for her bra.

I'm putting my shorts back on when I hear a strange alarm.

"Oh, crap! It's my alarm. I gotta go."

Victoria starts spinning around in place, frantic.

I place my hands on her shoulders and settle her down after handing her the bra I recently removed. I kiss the top of her head—a gesture meant to calm and focus her. She responds by lifting her chin and kissing my lips gently.

"Come on, let's get you home."

After putting Mariette's office to rights, I assist her with gathering her things from the studio and walk her to the door. "I'll see you in the morning at your grandparent's place, okay?"

"That's not too far for you?"

"Nah, closer to O'Hare." I don't know if it is or not, and frankly, I don't care.

"You have the address?"

"Yes, you gave it to me twice."

We kiss several more times, basically making out against the doorjamb, until the alarm goes off again. She finally steps out of my embrace.

"Okay, good night, Max."

"Good night, Miss Awkward."

Funny, she didn't say thanks. First time that's happened. Honestly, I think I should be thanking *her*.

Chapter 11

Fly Away

When Victoria said she lived at her family's house in Oak Brook, I assumed she meant a regular suburban home with three or four bedrooms and a barbecue in the backyard, not a fucking estate with a two-mile lane to a circular driveway that could hold enough cars to fill a small used-car lot. Not that any of the four cars in this driveway are used. *Fuck.* The only thing older than this year's model is Victoria's bike, Mikhail.

I knew she came from money, but fuuuuck, there's a Rolls parked out front! AWK Steel must be doing okay. I park my twelve-year-old Toyota next to her bike and look in the rearview. Hair's okay—a little shaggy but passable. Nothing in my teeth. I purposely wore my newest, plainest, unripped jeans and my button up. If I showed up in my regular clothes, it might not be too impressive. *Regular clothes*? Who am I kidding? I live in my well-worn dancewear, tank tops, sweats and shorts. Other than that, I have one suit that Mariette bought me for openings, three pairs of jeans and my one dress shirt. The one I'm wearing.

When I finally get up to the massive front door and raise my fist to knock, the door opens suddenly.

Victoria stands in the doorway but doesn't open the door quite all the way. Her hair is a low ponytail draped over one shoulder, and she's wearing a light pink sleeveless dress with a full skirt. She appears much younger without the severe bun, black dance wear and jean jacket. The only thing that's the same is the signature black-and-white Converse. I smile when I see them and shake my head.

"Hey, Max."

"Hi!"

"So, I'm all ready to go. Let me just grab my bag."

I make a move toward the door. "Let me help you."

"No, that's okay. I got it. I'm just going to say good-bye to my grandma and grandpa, and I'll be right out."

I start to protest when a hand appears on the door above Victoria's head and pulls it open further. Slightly behind her is an older couple, probably in their sixties. The woman is tiny. She has striking platinum hair, styled in what I can only guess is a very expensive modern cut, and large, round white glasses. She reminds me a bit of a photo negative Edna Mode from *The Incredibles*. The man is at least a foot taller than she is and has dark brown hair that's perfect. George Clooney perfect. Their appearance screams of money and breeding, and I'm suddenly all too conscious that my lower-class upbringing in the DOT is showing.

"Victoria! Why are you being rude?" the older woman lightly swats Miss Awkward on the arm. "Invite your friend in. Introduce us."

Victoria bugs out her eyes at me. "Of course, Grandmother. Come in, Max."

I step into the foyer. I'm sure this is a foyer because it doesn't look like any front hall I've ever been in.

"Hello, I'm Max." I shake the man's hand and then the woman's.

"Max. These are my grandparents, Kandis and Jerome Awkward. Grandma, Grandpa, this is Maximilian Devereaux."

Mrs. Awkward comes over and hugs me. I'm surprised at first, but I tentatively hug her back.

"Ooooh, I know very well who Mr. Devereaux is. His reputation precedes him."

Shit! Grandma Awkward knows about my reputation? This really *is* awkward.

"You do?" Victoria and I ask in unison.

"Yes, I've seen him dance. I've been to a lot of

99

Gallant ballets, of course, and your mother has told me how wonderful he is."

"She has?" We say simultaneously again.

Then I remember. I've met the Awkwards before at the last couple of season opening parties. Of course, I only engaged with them briefly because I'm a fucking idiot who thinks with his dick, and I was chasing Gia or Svetlana or some other dancer at the time. I was not giving my attention to an older couple who meant nothing to me. My recent past is becoming increasingly embarrassing to me.

"Mrs. Awkward—"

"Kandis, darling. Mrs. Awkward was my mother-in-law."

"Kandis, we have met before at a few of the Gallant parties."

"I know, dear, but you were rather distracted. I believe there was a Russian girl you were busy with."

"Yes, that." I shake my head and roll my eyes at my own ridiculousness.

Kandis takes my hands in hers. "We were all young and foolish once, Mr. Devereaux."

"Max." I insist.

"Okay, Max!" She reaches up and grips my bicep. "Oh, my."

Mr. Awkward steps forward and interrupts. "Kandis, stop ogling the boy. Max, it's good to meet you again. We are very excited for Victoria's opportunity with Gallant and your ballet." I like him immediately. He has a firm handshake, kind eyes and he doesn't smell of whiskey. The exact opposite of my father.

"I am, too, sir. She's very talented."

"Comes by it naturally, her father and moth—"

Victoria abruptly steps between us. "Grandpa, Max and I really need to go. You don't want us to miss our flight."

"Oh, no, no. You two head out."

We gather Victoria's suitcase and carry-on and make our way out to the car.

"Bye-bye, have fun in the Big Apple."

"We will," I say to reassure her grandmother. I plan on this being a very fun and memorable weekend.

"Victoria, why don't you invite Max to our party next weekend?'

"We'll see, Grandma!" Victoria shouts back.

"Call us. And your mother. Don't forget to call your mother."

"I won't. Bye."

"Bye now."

Her mother? The Mrs. Awkward I haven't met yet? Is she here? Perhaps this is the perfect time to introduce myself. "Can I meet your mother?"

"Well, you could… If she were here. She, uhm… she left right before you arrived."

"Your mother was just here?"

"Yes."

With a laugh, I ask, "And you didn't ask her to wait? Are you that embarrassed of me?"

Victoria averts her gaze as we walk away and flips her hand to dismiss the idea. "No. No, no, not at all."

"The lady doth protest too much."

"More Shakespeare, Max?"

"What can I say—he's my go-to guy for quotes."

Victoria plants her little hand on my shoulder, stopping both of us, and turns me toward her. She looks me straight in the eye. "Don't worry, you'll meet her soon enough."

I shrug, shake my head and kiss the top of her hand on my shoulder. I have to take Victoria's word on this one, and really, what am I in a hurry for? I already know my reputation precedes me with the other Mrs. Awkward.

Clicking the button on the key fob, I unlock the doors to my Corolla when we near the car. "It's open. I got this." I hold up Victoria's suitcase and make my way to the back of the car. I place her suitcase in the trunk next to mine. A brief shiver of excitement runs through me as I fantasize momentarily about how the weekend could play out personally and professionally.

When I take the driver's seat and put my sunglasses on, I point up to where Victoria's grandparents are still perched by the front door.

102

"They're adorable. What's this party I'm going to?"

"You really want to go? It's their wedding vow renewal and anniversary. Fifty years. You don't have to come if you think it's lame."

"You're kidding. They don't look old enough to have been married that long."

Victoria looks out the window and waves at them. "They were very, very young."

"And yet they lasted this long."

Victoria quiets as we pull through the circular drive and head out for the airport. I reach over and take her small hand.

"It's not lame," I tell her. "It's inspiring. I hope to have that someday." I can't believe I'm verbalizing these thoughts. Never in a million years could I imagine even having them.

Victoria slips her own sunglasses on, smiles and squeezes my hand.

I put my hand back on the steering wheel and shake my head. *Jeez, who am I?* Who is this person who's been talking of "real homes" and "enduring love?" It's like I don't know myself anymore.

I need to watch it. I'm losing my edge.

———

Staying quiet on the drive to the airport is the only mechanism I can employ to keep from spouting another girly emotional declaration. I'm mute as we park at O'Hare, check our bags, make our way through security and onto our flight for LaGuardia. Mariette purchased our tickets and had them sent to my phone. First Class. Yet another experience I've never had before.

It's not until we're seated and offered orange juice or champagne that I feel secure enough with my shit to interact with Victoria again. I need to be more careful with my words. And what better way than to channel my douchebag side.

"Why don't you want to change your last name?" I've asked her dozens of times but have never gotten her to give me a real reason.

"You're not going to get off this, are you? Not until I tell you?"

"No."

"It's my dad's real last name, even though he shortened it for his job."

Finally, she's starting to trust me enough to tell me more about her family. Maybe I can get her to reveal a bit more. "Didn't he work in the family business?"

"No, he was an artist. Grandma and Grandpa didn't approve. At least not at first."

"You never really talk about him. I mean, since you told me that Mikhail used to belong to him. Where is he now?"

Victoria smiles, but her eyes are sad and faraway looking. "You remembered. About

Mikhail. He died. When I was little."

Jesus. I'm an asshole. I take her hand. "I didn't know. I'm sorry."

"It's okay. There's no way you could have known. It was a while ago."

"Confession time. I Googled you, Victoria."

"What?"

"I know you're not interested in Insta-snap or Face-Tweet or whatever. Neither am I. I wanted to know more about you, so I Googled you."

"And?"

"All I could find was pictures of you and your grandparents. I couldn't find a picture of your parents at all."

"Mother and Father are—were—very private people. He was a private person."

"I really am sorry."

"It's okay. I just wish I could have had him around longer." There's a hitch in her voice. Tears are forming in her eyes.

I hand her the cocktail napkin I got with my drink. Trying my best to lighten the mood, I say, "Victoria's a long name. If you won't let me change Awkward, can I at least call you by a nickname? Do you have a nickname?"

"Yeah, I do, but it was my parent's special name for me. It's sort of sacred."

I'm intrigued. It can't be that precious. How many nicknames are there for Victoria?

"Can I at least shorten it? Call you Vic? Or

Tori?"

"Really, Max. What's in a name?"

"You're quoting Shakespeare to me? Seriously, Victoria?"

"I'm just messing with you. Vic's okay. I like Vic."

After patting her eyes, she leans back in the seat, turns her face toward me and grins wickedly and says, "But not in front of anyone else. Not in front of the company." Just like I told her all those weeks ago.

Chapter 12

New York, New York, Big City of
Dreams

W̲e disembark the plane and make
our way down the concourse. At
the end of the walkway is a bulky
guy in a dark suit, black slicked-back hair and
mirrored sunglasses on the top of his head. He's
holding a placard that says DEVEREAUX.

Vic giggles. "I guess that's our limo driver."
She seems accustomed to it.

"Limo?" I've only seen guys holding signs in
the airport in movies.

We approach the man. "Uhm… Hi."

"Hello, sir," he says in a thick New York
accent. "Mr. Max Devereaux?"

"Yes, I'm Max Devereaux and this is Victoria
Awkward."

"Nice to meet you, Mr. Devereaux. Welcome
back, Miss Awkward. I'm Tommy. I'll be your

driver for the weekend. If you'll follow me, I have your limo waiting right outside."

Evidently, Tommy and Vic are acquainted. We move to follow him, but he slides around next to Victoria and takes the handle of her carry-on. "Let me just get the young lady's suitcase."

Victoria allows him to take it, and we proceed out of the terminal. A shiny black limousine is parked at the curb.

I turn to Victoria and mouth, "*Wow!*"

She appears unfazed but smiles appreciatively. This must be no big deal to someone raised with so much wealth.

Tommy puts our cases in the trunk. Once we're seated comfortably in the spacious leather backseat, he gets in. Tommy slides open the partition between the front and back of the limo. "You're staying at The Standard, right? High Line, not East Village."

I'm a bit stunned he knows, but I'm beginning to sense Mariette had everything arranged to the letter. First class. Limo. Driver for the weekend. I'm guessing The Standard won't be on the same level as a Motel 6.

I check the itinerary Mariette sent to my phone. "Yes, The Standard High Line."

"You're in for a treat. The Standard is where all the celebrities stay. That's the place Beyonce and Jay Z got in that fight with her sister in the elevator. You know the video that was all over the

TV?"

Victoria and I nod, and I say, "Uh-huh."

Tommy just keeps chattering away. "They got a nightclub at the Top of The Standard that people call the Boom Boom Room. I hear it's quite a party."

"We're here on business. I doubt we'll get up there," Victoria informs him. "Besides, I'm not twenty-one yet."

"Ha! Pardon my forwardness, miss, but you're so pretty the bouncer wouldn't even card you. That's a 'pretty people' place. You two are perfect."

Victoria blushes all over when she tells him, "Thank you." She is gorgeous.

It constantly surprises me that she's embarrassed when someone mentions her beauty. Wrapping my arm around her waist, I slide her closer to me. I keep shifting my gaze between her and the window to catch the sights. I've never been to New York before. I get a glimpse of Roosevelt Island just as we go into a tunnel. It's a bit of a drive to our hotel from the airport, but I don't mind, I've got Vic by my side and lots of new things to see.

Eventually, Tommy pulls up in front of a building that consists of two hinged glass monoliths straddling an abandoned elevated train track. "Here we are—The Standard. They call it the High Line because that's the name of the old rail line it's built over. Now it's a park. A two-mile-long park above the city streets. A nice one, too."

This is a long way from the crappy complex I lived in with my parents and sisters in Dorchester. A *long* way.

I try to tip Tommy, but he won't have it. "Nah, Mr. D. It's okay if I call you that? Right?"

"Absolutely."

He gets the bags from the trunk and takes them into the hotel, letting us know they'll be in our room when we get there. Then he hands me his card and says, "Call me anytime you need transportation. I'm on call for you for the entire weekend. Twenty-four hours a day."

This is overwhelming. Mariette has gone all out to make sure we are very well cared for. I've never had an issue with how hard I work at Gallant or the hours. It's my life. This trip is a surprising perk.

Upon checking in at the desk, the manager comes out and personally escorts us to our accommodations. When we reach a door that says Liberty on it, he says, "Enjoy. And please let me know if you need anything." He hands us two keycards.

This can't be right. Victoria and I look at the cards in our hands and then each other.

The manager is almost at the elevator when I ask, "Shouldn't there be two rooms?"

Without really looking back he explains, "It's a suite. Ms. Gallant arranged it." The elevator opens the moment he touches the button to call it, and he steps in before I'm able to interrogate him further.

A suite. Wow! I've never been in a suite. One more thing to add to my memories of this trip. If Mariette arranged this, it probably has two bedrooms. By the time I've turned around, Victoria has opened the door and entered the suite. I step in behind her and place my hand on her lower back.

A large exhalation escapes her, followed by a quick gasp. "Oh!"

The suite is massive with floor-to-ceiling windows that frame stunning views of the Hudson River looking all the way down to Ellis Island and the Statue of Liberty. We don't move so much as spin in place, taking in every detail. Very quickly we discover there are not two bedrooms since both our suitcases are placed right below a platform with an impressive round king-size bed in the adjacent bedroom area. One gigantic bed and one enormous wooden teacup-shaped soaking tub.

I'm confused and delighted and, frankly, suddenly feeling dirty and in need of a bath. Even though this suite is a player's dream come true, the remaining fragment of my conscience whispers, *"This can't be right. I don't think this is what Mariette had in mind when she ordered a suite."*

My next thought is, "*Fuck it!*"

Victoria walks past me, making a beeline for the tub with nothing on but her bra and panties. She reaches around with both hands, unhooks her black-lace-over-nude bra and throws it back at me. I catch it and stare at it like it's a fabric invitation to fun. When I look up, she's reached the tub. She flips her hair over her shoulder and glances back at me while bending to turn on the water. "I need to freshen up. Care to join me, Mr. Devereaux?" She sweetens the deal by shimmying out of her matching panties and kicking them off her feet.

"Ah, the hell with Mariette. If this suite is a mistake, then it's her fault, not mine. Let's get clean, Vic. And then dirty." My inner bad boy's voice of reason has finally found his power of speech.

Victoria beckons me over by crooking her index finger at me and then steps into the tub. Still standing, she watches me rip off my jacket, shirt, belt, pants and underwear on my way to her. I admire her in all her nakedness, framed by the scenery in the window behind her. Someone in New Jersey with a telescope is certainly getting one hell of a peep show right now. It doesn't bother me one bit. Victoria doesn't seem fazed. I hope our Peeping Tom, whoever he may be, is getting a colossal spankfest out of this.

I step into the tub and run one finger along her jawline. She lifts her chin and opens her mouth slightly. Her tongue slides out between her lips. She runs it over her lower lip. My dick seems to be imagining it running along him because he springs even further to life from semi to full.

I trail my finger across Victoria's collarbone and continue down between her breasts. I detour my descent to run it around each of her peaked nipples.

Victoria sighs. Her head tips back and to the right, and her eyes close as she does. I keep my gaze on her face to watch her reaction. I'm about to slide my hand over her stomach and torment— what I'm sure is—her hot, wet clit when Victoria lifts her head, shakes it and then drops to her knees in the tub, causing a big splash. My balls are engulfed a tsunami of bathwater right before my cock is engulfed by the warmness of Victoria's mouth.

She scoops up some warm water and massages my balls while working my shaft with her other hand and her mouth. I rake my hands into her silky strawberry blonde tresses and grip handfuls down to the root. She gobbles me up all the way to the base without gagging and then slowly sucks me off to the tip before starting again. I groan loudly. On and on she repeats the movement, adding a swirl of her tongue around my tip at the end. I'm going to blow any minute.

"Victoria, baby. I need you to stop."

She pops off my dick with loud suck and pouts

up at me. "Really?"

"I didn't say I want you to stop. Trust me. But I really want to be inside you, and I can't do that if you make me come."

Victoria's frown changes to a huge grin. "All right, then." She surprises me again by grabbing one of my ass cheeks, splaying her other hand over my lower abdomen and pushing me back into the tub. My dick screams to be touched again.

Reaching up, I cup my hands around her hips. Victoria straddles me, lines herself up with my dick and slowly mounts me. I push my dick up into the tight, hot, wet undulation. It feels like perfection.

Victoria slides her hands up my arms and around my neck, twisting her fingers into the hair at my nape. I rotate my thumb against her throbbing clit and simultaneously lave the nipple of her left tit with my wanting mouth as she rocks while sighing, moaning and purring.

Victoria rocks and rocks, repeatedly humming and singing, "Yes, yes, yes." Suddenly her back arches, her hands grip my shoulders and I know she's about to come like a freight train. I fuck into her with all I have, and it tips her over the edge. She takes me with her. I'm sure there's water everywhere around the tub.

Once we catch our breath, I pull out and realize—no protection.

"Oh my God, Vic. I didn't use a condom.

Jesus, I'm sorry."

Staying straddled over me, Victoria places a finger over my lips. "Sshh. No worries. I'm on the pill."

"Oh, thank God."

"Yeah, I thought it might be a good idea."

"You are as smart as you are beautiful."

I grab a washcloth from the side of the tub, dunk it to wet it and then pour some of the hotel's body wash on it. I work it up into a nice foam and begin to wash Victoria's shoulders and chest.

"Max, that smells really good. It reminds me of a smell from my childhood. Weird. I haven't smelled that in so long."

I check out the bottle. "It's Patchouli Lavender Vanilla."

"That's it. Patchouli. My dad wore that."

I cough at the mention of her father.

"I'm sorry. I guess I shouldn't talk about my dad while we're naked and just… you know."

I need to get this conversation out of daddy world. "The bottle says it's from Israel. I should buy some."

"Nice segue out of that awkward moment." Victoria leans over and kisses me on the forehead and then down the side of my face by my ear. She whispers hotly, "Mmhmm. You should buy some. And give me a bath with it every day."

"Deal."

Victoria and I are clad in fluffy white hotel robes, standing with her back to my front in front of the floor-to-ceiling windows in our suite and watching the boats go up and down the Hudson River as the sun sets. I wrap my arms tighter around her slim waist, nuzzle the crook of her neck and cover it with small kisses.

"Want to go out? There's a great big city out there."

"No, I'd rather stay in with you. Order something up and then go over the choreography." Victoria turns in my arms and looks over my shoulder into the living room. "There's enough room here. We just have to push the table out of the way."

"Are you sure?"

"Yes, we can go out tomorrow night after the workshop. I should be asking you that question anyway. I've been to New York before. I used to live nearby when I was little. It's your first time."

"I'm fine staying in and rehearsing. Now, what should we eat? I'm starving."

Victoria lifts my arm and ducks under it to go over to the desk and find the menu. Even bundled up in the much too large robe that gives her the appearance of being swallowed by a polar bear, she is graceful and sexy.

"I'll order for us," Victoria says as she picks up the phone and presses a single button.

I remove my robe and grab my favorite gray sweat shorts from my suitcase. I listen to her order as I put them on.

"Yes, the Liberty Suite. We'd like the kale and endive salad, the diver scallops and the New York rib eye. Medium rare." She calls to me. "Is medium rare okay, Max?"

"Perfect." My mouth waters, either from her ordering or the way she just said my name.

She continues, "Yes, medium rare. Uhm, asparagus. And some sparkling water. Oh, and some kind of chocolate desert. Whatever the chef chooses. Thank you."

Hanging up the phone, she sighs. "Now, I'm really hungry. Dinner should be here in fifteen or twenty minutes. I should change."

"No, stay in your robe. I want you to relax. You can put on something when we rehearse. Vic? Can I tell you something?"

"What?"

"You are the sexiest orderer I've ever met. I got a boner just listening to you say endive and diver scallops."

Victoria giggles and runs and dives onto the round king bed, twisting as she does and landing flat on her back. "Max, you're hilarious. I was ordering dinner, not reading porn."

I look down at her from where I stand next to

the bed. She's sprawled out and her bathrobe has worked its way open. I can see one of her breasts heaving with her laughter and a hint of pussy. "Works like porn for me."

She holds both her arms up and beckons me like a baby asking to be picked up. "Come here."

I comply readily. Who am I to refuse some pre-dinner foreplay?

———————

Dinner was unbelievable! I was working so hard to be cool. I didn't reveal to Vic that I'd never had room service in my life until now. Letting her feed me scallops and bites of chocolate cake evoked a kind of nurturing I'd never experienced as a child. Being with her was satisfying sexually and, I was coming to realize, emotionally.

Victoria leaned back in the chair and patted her now slightly pooched tummy. "I'm so full. Look at this food baby. I don't think I can dance."

"That's okay. Let's just get up and walk through a few sections I'm unsure of." I stand and pull her up from the chair. Victoria still in her robe, we walk and talk through the opening, skip to the chase sequence and run through a segment near the end. In the final movements, when Victoria walks across the room and into my arms, she melts into me. She's tired. I lift her up with both arms and cradle her against me.

"This isn't part of the choreography."

"I know, but you're obviously wrung out. Let's go to bed." I walk toward the bed, turning off lights along the way.

Victoria turns and yawns against my chest before looking up at me. "You'll get no argument from me."

I carry her to the bed and place her gently on it. She wiggles under the covers, pats the space next to her and turns away from me toward the windows overlooking the river.

"You sure? Remember, no bed sex?"

"We aren't having sex."

I slide in behind her and pull her back flush against me. We look out the window and watch the lights across on the Jersey side and the boats moving below.

My first time in bed with Miss Awkward isn't to bang her senseless because we're so exhausted. We fall sleep in each other's arms, and I'm not disappointed at all.

Chapter 13

Workshop

I wake up gradually, mirroring the slowness of the morning light coming through the expansive windows in the suite. I'm hugging something, but it's not Victoria. It's a pillow. I prop up on one elbow and run my hand through my hair when I spy her across the room, holding a cup of coffee and looking out over the Hudson.

She stands completely still and dressed like Madonna: lace scarf in her loosely curled hair, black capri tights, Ray-Bans, red lipstick and denim jacket.

She turns. "I couldn't find a green lame jacket, but what do you think of this?" She *chaînés* slowly over to me, stops with her back to me and looks over her shoulder.

She's appliquéd a replica of the sparkly pyramid from Susan's character's jacket onto hers. She did that. For the ballet. For the workshop. For me.

"Come here."

"No," she scolds, shaking her head and wagging a finger at me. "You need to get up and get in the shower. We need to get there early and warm up." She throws the covers off my naked body. Her robe and my sweats came off during the night, but we didn't fuck. Hmm, *fuck* doesn't describe what I want to do with her in this bed. No, I want to consume her, possess her, worship her.

Dare I think it? I want to make love to her.

I address the small gathering in the rehearsal space at the American Ballet Theatre. The "small gathering" is made up of big names—all the best choreographers and artistic directors of the most important ballet companies in New York. I acknowledge my nervousness only to myself and then find "arrogant Max" to do the speaking.

"Thank you all for coming today. You've all seen the movie *Desperately Seeking Susan*?" Heads nod around the room. "This is an abbreviated version of my vision of it as a ballet. I'll be dancing all the male parts. Miss Victoria Awkward will be performing the roles of Roberta and Susan. My only bit of direction is please pay attention to the jacket. The jacket is key. It starts with Susan, gets sold, gets saved by Roberta and, through a series of crazy dance sequences, finds its way back to Susan."

I walk back to the audio system. Vic is standing next to it. I take her hand and squeeze it while pinning her with my gaze. She knows this workshop, and the buzz it could create means the world to me.

She gives me a small smile and says softly, "*Merde!*" The ballet good luck word. What is "shit" to everyone in France is "good luck" to us.

"*Merde!*" I start the music with flick of the remote, and we begin.

Victoria is flawless. She hits every mark and nails every sequence. Fuck, I'm the one dancing with her, and *I'm* mesmerized. When we end the twenty-minute presentation with the characters of Dez and Roberta finally seeing each other for real, life imitates art and I finally get it. It all becomes clear. Everything I've pushed down or denied about how I feel about Victoria hits me right in the center of my heart. I can't break eye contact with her.

I'm only brought out of the moment by the copious applause in the room and a few of our audience up on their feet.

"Gorgeous, really lots of potential."

"If Mariette passes, ABT will take it."

A voice from across the room rises above all the rest. "That's if I don't snap it up first."

Victoria and I both turn in place. A tall blond

man with a bit of an accent and amazing posture fills the doorframe to the rehearsal space. It's Madsen. Peter Madsen. From the New York Ballet. I'd know him anywhere. The man has been my hero since I was a kid. Him and Baryshnikov.

Madsen steps forward with long strides. "And Max, you'd be a fool not to cast her. Sorry, I didn't even introduce myself, Peter Madsen—"

"Of the New York Ballet," I say, cutting him off and finishing his introduction. "No introduction needed, sir. I'm Max Devereaux from Gallant."

"Also, no need. Mariette has told me all about you. And you, miss?"

Victoria giggles.

Madsen regards Victoria. "What part would you prefer, Roberta or Susan?"

Victoria looks at the floor. Madsen lifts her chin with a long finger and stares her down.

"Uh, Roberta."

Really? I thought she would have said Susan.

Madsen continues while still gazing at Victoria. "You've really got something here, Max." *Is he talking about the ballet or Vic*? Because he's right on both accounts.

I just didn't realize it until just now how much I loved my creation and Miss Awkward. It took really seeing her and having another man point it out.

I'm in love with Victoria Awkward.

123

Chapter 14

First Date

We spend the remainder of the presentation and workshop taking suggestions from our audience. Brilliant, nuanced choreography and grand production ideas alike. It is dizzying to be in the middle of this discussion about something I've created. To hear others' effusive praise and excitement. It's also difficult because I cannot stop looking at Victoria.

She really is a beauty, an original and mine—at least for now. I have no idea how to make that continue. We've made no promises about what happens after we finish *Desperately*. Rehearsals will start for the season. There is the very real possibility that she will be too busy for me, or worse, she'll be swept away by some other guy.

My mind bounces between the discussions and my internal turmoil over this girl. I have no reference for being in love. *How do I do this?*

There is no ballet or boxing class to teach me this.

Before we leave the rehearsal, Madsen calls Victoria over to him.

I am very surprised to see them hug. Then he gives her a kiss on both cheeks. They speak for a moment. As I walk over to say good-bye and shake my idol's hand, I catch the tail end of their conversation.

"Tell her I miss her. Give her my best."

Give who his best?

Madsen looks up as I approach and reaches out to me. "Devereaux, I expect to be invited to opening night."

"Absolutely, sir."

———

Tommy picks us up in the limo. On the way back to the hotel, I quiz Victoria.

"Who was Madsen giving his best to?"

"Ah, uhm... my... Ma... Mariette. He was telling me to give our regards to Mariette." She seems flustered.

"And he seemed awfully familiar, hugging you."

"He was just giving me his congratulations. It was kind of intimidating. Why all the questions, Max? Jealous of a man twice your age?"

I laugh it off, but yes, I am jealous. He's Peter-fucking-Madsen, and I'm in love with her. I can't stop myself thinking about it. Dancing and fucking have been the primary preoccupations of my brain for a good portion of my life. This feels entirely different and daunting.

Getting to the suite, I'm antsy. I'm at a loss for what to say, so I pace.

Victoria drops her dance bag on the floor with her familiar thud.

"Max, you're really keyed up. I'm going to take a shower. You're welcome to join me."

Her voice tempts me, but I've gone all cerebral. If I get in the shower with her, I'll cave and spill my guts. She could reject me. *That* would make for a pleasant trip home. No, I need to think this through.

"You go ahead. I need to make some calls. I'll shower after you, and then we can talk about tonight."

Vic shrugs. "Okay, whatever you like."

I hear her in the shower singing The Cure's "Just Like Heaven." She's horribly off-key, and it's charming. She isn't perfect after all, but even her imperfectness is perfect to me. My quirky 80s-loving girl. My girl. I need to make her mine, not just my dance partner and sex partner, but really mine.

After making a few calls to the concierge, I have a plan for our evening. As I go to take my shower, I pass Victoria, who's clad in just a fluffy white towel, and say, "Wear something you'll be comfortable in outside and shoes you can walk in."

She stops me and kisses me on the nose. "I'm intrigued, and I have just the outfit and shoes."

From the bathroom, I yell, "You're not kidding anyone, Awkward! I know you're going to wear those Converse!"

She pops her head into the bathroom and runs her gaze up and down my now naked body. "Admit it. You love them."

"I do," I admit with ease. *And I love you, Victoria Awkward.* That I do *not* say out loud.

I take a quick shower so as not to linger and think too much. As I enter the bedroom, I rub my head with a towel and have another towel around my waist. I don't get far into the room before Victoria throws some clothes onto the bed.

"I took the liberty of selecting a few things for you."

Victoria got it just right. Ripped jeans, a black polo and flip flops.

She looks like she's ready to attend Coachella. Naturally beautiful with her copper kissed hair in a braid to one side, shorts and a tank top that shows her pert nipples. She topped it with a fringed kimono-style jacket. If she's wearing makeup, it's minimal and probably unnecessary. Her skin glows in the light filtering through the windows. Her lips are shiny and pouty.

"Hurry up. I'm getting hungry."

I'm already hungry—for her.

"How do you know we're eating?"

"We better be, or I will officially declare this date crappy."

She said "date." Maybe she feels the same.

I dress rapidly and run fingers through my hair. "Don't worry. We are definitely eating." I move to her and scoop her up against my chest. "Ready?"

"Yes."

"I gotta confess. I'm a little revved up from the day." I'm totally putting it mildly. "Do you mind if we walk the High Line?"

"I was hoping we'd get to do that. I've been anxious to explore it. I read about it when they started fixing it." Victoria grabs a floppy felt hat and her sunglasses on the way out the door, completing her music festival Bohemian-chic look.

The abandoned elevated railroad track that The Standard straddles is a now a nearly two-mile linear public park called the High Line with art, plantings, water features and moveable chaise longues on wheels that roll along the old train tracks. It also runs right through Chelsea Market, which is where I take Victoria. When we enter, I know the concierge did me a solid. It's a food wonderland. Seriously, foodie heaven.

"I thought we could pick up some bread, cheese, cured meats and wine and find a place on the High Line to eat."

"Good idea. It will be good to be outside after being in the studio all day."

We slowly amble from store to store, getting all the components of our dinner. I pick up some plates, cups and plasticware at one of the shops. They give me a basket to collect everything in. Victoria looks through the wide selection of cheeses and selects a few.

When she puts the cheeses in the basket, I slip my arm around her waist, pull her to me and duck down to kiss her cheek. "This is fun."

"You've never gone shopping?"

"Not with anyone. I just grab the same things over and over at the shop by my apartment. I'm embarrassed to say I don't really do dates. This is new to me."

"Is the mighty Max Devereaux becoming domesticated?"

Domesticated. Infatuated. Whipped. Call it what you will. "Something like that."

No. Max Devereaux has just become aware of what's important to him. Now to find a way to tell her. And hope she doesn't laugh in my face or reject me. Her actions make me think she might care for me, too. But she's never put it into words.

With our findings, we walk farther up the High

Line and find a table with a large umbrella situated between two planters. Secluded enough to be intimate. It looks out over the Hudson. We talk and laugh and eat. Our conversation is frivolous and not related to work. I don't do that too often—talk about things not related to dance. We giggle and comment on passersby. The High Line is excellent for people watching. Victoria feeds me cheese and I sneak her sips of the cool, crisp German Riesling the sommelier at the wine store recommended. Time with her expands and contracts. I want to capture every moment like a movie so I can play it again, but it rushes by too quickly for my liking.

As the sun begins to set, we leisurely make our way back to our hotel hand in hand. The sun provides a light design like I've never seen in any play or dance production. I swear there is a special lamp from the sky shining down on us. In said production, this would be the time to declare my feelings, but I don't. I chicken out. And I want to talk to someone first. Mariette. Not to tell her of my love for Victoria. She'll figure that out soon enough. No, I want to break the bet. I want to be done with all of that. So, verbalizing how much I care for her must wait, but showing her will not. Not at all.

Chapter 15

Bed

"Max, that was amazing. Probably the best date ever."

"Best date ever? Whoa! I'm in trouble. Where do I possibly go from there?"

"Really, I loved it. I love…" She hesitates, and then she pulls her hat off, throws it onto the couch and launches herself into my arms. *What was she going to say? That she loves me?* Maybe I'm not the only one struggling to come out with it.

The only light in the room comes from the setting sun through the windows. In minutes, it will be dark and the twinkling lights of the city and reflections sparkling on the river will be dancing on the ceiling. I want to share that with her.

"I know you said no bed sex, Victoria, but it seems a waste to be here with you in this gorgeous room after the day we've had and not have you in that big, round bed."

"The Austin Powers bed?"

Beautiful, talented and funny. I chuckle, pull

her tighter into my arms and smile. "Is that what you're calling it?"

"Yes, who else has a round bed? Nobody that I know."

"Okay, then the Austin Powers bed it is. Yeah, baby, yeah!" I haven't said that catch phrase in ages.

Victoria slaps me playfully on the chest and tells me, "Oh, behave."

"Never," I whisper as I catch her hand and crash my lips to hers. We go from silly to serious in one point two seconds.

I move her arms up and around my neck, slide my hands down her stomach, around her hips to grab her tight-as-fuck ass and lift her to my waist. She wraps her legs around my waist and right above my ever-growing cock.

"Oh!" she exclaims when she feels it and commands, "Take me to bed, Max, or lose me forever."

Oooh, *Top Gun* reference.

"As you wish." I counter with *The Princess Bride*.

We can't seem to stop with the movie lines, although we've wisely switched to more romantically themed films.

I walk with Victoria firmly in my grip and then turn and sit down on the edge of the bed with her straddling me. Now I can feel the warmth of her core right on my dick. As I take her face in my hands and bring her lips to mine, she rocks her pelvis against me, her shorts and my jeans causing all manner of friction.

Victoria's hands skate down the front of my polo before she tugs it up, moving her hands up my abs and chest and over my shoulders, breaking the kiss to undress my upper body.

With our faces and lips close again, she whispers, "I love the feel of your body, Max. I love feeling it right now, and I love the way it feels when we dance together."

I plant small kisses all around her mouth and cheeks as she speaks while slipping her kimono top and tank top off to cup her breasts. "I. Feel. Exactly. The. Same. Goddamn, your breasts are perfect."

"Really? Not too big? Somebody once said they were too big for a ballerina."

"No, just right. They fit my hands perfectly. That somebody is an idiot." *Who the fuck is talking about her breasts*?

I run my arm around her and up her back and lean her torso away from me. She gracefully follows and arches back with her arms over her head in *first* position. I take one of her breasts into my mouth. I hold it gently and massage as I power her nipple deep and then swirl my tongue around and around the pebbled peak. My dick hardens with each circumnavigation, each moan she makes

133

in response and her growing heat against me. I lavish the same attention on her other breast. Victoria's moans become louder. She sounds like she does when she's about to come. I'd love to push her over the edge, but not yet.

Suddenly, she stops. Stops moving and stops moaning.

"No, not yet," she says to herself as much as me.

She removes herself from my lap, stands in front of me and unbuttons my jeans. I'm not wearing underwear, and my cock jumps out to greet her the second the last button is undone. She stands back and licks her lips hungrily in what I hope is anticipation.

"Back!" she commands as she points to the head of the bed behind me.

I shimmy back, losing my jeans the rest of the way. "As you wish."

"Oh, I have a lot of wishes."

I sit with my back against the headboard, my legs stretched out in front of me and my dick hard as granite, vibrating and slapping my lower abs, almost beckoning her all on its own.

"You know the best way to get wishes?" she asks as she steps out of her shorts, leaving on her teeny, tiny, pink-and-black panties and crawling up to me from the end of the bed.

"No, how?"

"Like you do with birthday candles." Victoria

has seated herself to the side of me near my thigh. She encircles the base of my dick with her small, strong hand. "Blow on it." Victoria dips her head and kisses the top of my dick, before taking the whole thing in her mouth. As she sucks, blows and sweeps her tongue up and down my shaft, my vision swirls. My hands are grasping the headboard and then twisting the sheets. I reach for her and slide my fingers between her lower stomach and her panties and find her soaking wet core. I slip one and then another finger into her and curve them rhythmically against the spot over and over while my thumb works her clit as she grinds into my palm.

Vic moans with my cock in her mouth, and I swear I almost lose it right down her pretty throat.

My turn to stop the madness. Reluctantly, I take my fingers from her, but not without removing her panties as I retreat. I throw them off the bed and they smack against the window. They'd be in New Jersey if the window wasn't there.

I lift her head from my lap, already missing the feeling of the end of her braid tickling my thigh.

"What?" she asks.

"We're doing this together, not alone. Okay?"

"O-okay."

She comes up in a tall kneel and is about to climb on when I have the overwhelming desire to taste her.

When she swings her leg over, I scoot down so my mouth is right in line with her and pull her onto me. I lick her softly and taste her.

"Max, oh my God, I thought you were—"

Victoria stops in mid-sentence. She leans forward to use the headboard for stability. As I lick and suck and devour her, stroking my tongue up and down her folds, circling and powerfully taking her clit, she rides my face, all the while purring and mewing.

Victoria stills, her thighs contract by my ears and then a glorious wave of her deliciousness floods my eager mouth. She screams out, and I lap even more fervently until she can take no more and pulls herself from my face, slides down my body and mounts my throbbing cock.

It's a tight velvety heaven inside her. I never want to be anywhere else.

As I take her hips, my hands are large enough that my thumbs are free to take slow measured strokes across her pink and blossoming clit. With each touch, she moans a little longer and a little louder.

I match each of her moans with my own growls while we rock into each other. Victoria throws her head back, and I sit up and pull her closer, thrusting my cheek against her breasts. Her body shivers, and she contracts around me, milking our shared pleasure, and I come immediately after her.

We slow and pant, and when we finally have

our wits about us, we touch foreheads and look deeply at one another for long minutes before she leaves my lap. I tuck her under my arm and kiss her head.

I look up at the ceiling. I was right. Lights from the river dance along the ceiling.

Victoria sighs and points to the ceiling. "Max, look at that. So beautiful." Just as I wished, we see it together.

———————

Breathing her scent in and out as I nuzzle into her hair, I say, "Victoria, tell me something. A secret. Tell me something that nobody else knows. Tell me something that makes you happy. The happiest you've ever been."

Victoria twists onto her stomach and rests her chin on my chest. "You make me happy."

I stroke her hair. "You make me happy, too. But before me. When you were little or something."

"My parents had a cottage on the ocean." Victoria turns over again onto her back and cuddles into me. She reaches over and intertwines her fingers with mine. "Well, the family still owns it, but now it belongs to me."

She owns a house. I own nothing.

"It's outside of New York City on Long Island,

right on the beach. They bought it to get away from their jobs in the city. They'd worked there since before I was born." She pauses for a moment and then, with thickness in her voice, adds, "Before my dad died."

I've wondered about her father. I hold her hand tighter. "I'm sorry."

"Thanks. It's okay."

I can't stop myself from kissing her head. The overwhelming desire to protect her and take away her pain washes over me.

"Before he died, I remember spending weekends out there. Just the three of us. That's probably when I fell in love with dancing. We'd all dance together in the kitchen with the windows open and the sea air all around us. That's why I'm not lonely when I dance. They're with me. Both of them."

"They were in the dance world?"

She nods against my shoulder. "Yes."

When she turns her face away from me and I feel her swallow a few times, I can tell she no longer wants to discuss it.

Rolling to my side, I whisper in her ear, "I'll let you in on a little secret. When I came to Gallant, I wasn't Max Devereaux."

"What? Who were you?"

"I was Max Delaney." I swallow a few times. "That's my real name. And I only *wish* my father had died."

"Don't say that."

"I've told you the things he said to me. What he called me."

"That's still no reason to wish someone dead. He's your father."

I continue, not even responding to her argument. "What I didn't tell you is he beat me so bad one time I had to go to the emergency room. These scars on my face aren't from falling off my bike, Vic." My voice catches. *Why the fuck am I getting emotional over my waste of a father?* "He was so cruel and controlling. He wouldn't let my mom or sisters visit me in the hospital."

"I'm so sorry, Max." Now it's her turn to hold me and comfort me.

"We never danced joyously in the kitchen. I don't have any memories of my parents or childhood like you do."

Victoria gently touches the scars on my chin and neck. "You'll make your own memories in the future."

God, I hope they're with her.

"And you know what the thing I'm proudest of is?"

She nods against me.

"That when I finally got out, got away from him, I didn't sneak out with my tail between my legs. No, I beat my father into unconsciousness and took off."

"But he's your father."

"I know, and I want nothing from him. Not even his name. That's my secret. I invented myself. My name isn't Max Delaney. It's Devereaux."

"I like your invention."

God, I love this woman. Please let her love me back.

"Max, let me tell you a secret." She moves her lips next to my ear and whispers, "I'm really, really happy. This weekend may become one of the happiest memories I have. I wish we could stay here forever."

Is this a declaration or a good-bye? I can't figure it out.

I turn and whisper back. "As much as I wish we could stay here forever, we need to get home. You have rehearsal tomorrow night." And I need to talk to Mariette. As soon as possible.

"Just one more day. It would be okay if I missed one. I'm just in the corps."

She doesn't know. *How can she not know*? My tone reveals my surprise, I'm sure. "You don't know?"

"Know what?"

"Darlin', you're cast as the sylph in *La Sylphide*."

Victoria stands. On the bed. Completely naked. Once again on show for Lower Manhattan and Hoboken. Her fair skin glowing, she jumps up and down and then falls to her knees and begins to cry. Big, fat tears of joy.

"Really?"

"Yes, really. I thought you knew."

"No, I didn't bother looking at the cast list. I just figured since I was new…"

"No, it's real. You've been cast as the sylph."

She flies into my arms and covers me with kisses, but even tired as we both are, I make slow sweet love to her again. In bed.

She was right. It's too intimate, and I don't want it ever to be any other way. And I don't want it to ever be with anyone else. Ever again.

Chapter 16

Big Reveal

When we board the plane, I text Mariette that I want to talk with her as soon as I arrive in Chicago. We agree to meet at Gino's East South Loop. It's near the studio, and it won't hurt to have a drink while we talk. I don't tell Victoria where I'm going. Doing so means explaining my relationship with Mariette and the bet, and I don't want to have to do that before I confess my feelings.

Victoria asks me to drop her off at the Waldorf. She's anxious to speak with her mother. She tells me she has a lot to tell her. I wonder if it's about me but rationalize that it's more likely about her lead role in *La Sylphide* this season.

I pull up in front of the Waldorf, and the doormen come rushing out. They quickly take Victoria's bags, and all too soon it's time for me to leave.

I rub my hands up and down her arms—neither of us making a move to disconnect—with our eyes locked on one another. "Can I see you later? After you talk to your mom?"

"Sure. I'll call you after I unpack and tell her all about the weekend."

"All? About the weekend?" I widen my eyes and raise my eyebrows toward my hairline.

Victoria gives me a gorgeous crooked smile and giggles. "OMG, I didn't even think about how that came out. No, no, not everything. Not the part about you and me. That's between us."

Not forever, I think to myself before bending down to kiss her. A soft, slow kiss that hopefully relays all the fullness of my heart for her. My hands start shaking ever so slightly. I want to scream to the heavens how I feel about her.

She steps back and away from me when we break. "Wow!"

"Yeah," I agree without even knowing what I'm agreeing to but guessing it was the power of the kiss.

"Good thing my mom didn't see that. I'd have a lot of explaining to do."

I step forward, and without touching her, I lean in and husk into her ear, "I don't care if she does see."

I turn and leave a wide-eyed Victoria standing on the sidewalk outside her home. I don't turn back around or make eye contact because I'm sure if I did, I'd never leave. Besides, I have a new mission. I can't get to Mariette fast enough to tell her the bet's off. I want to be able to tell the world that the Awkward girl is mine.

When I walk into Gino's East, Mariette is already there at a high four-top facing the door. A pizza and a pitcher of beer on the table. Her muscular legs are crossed with one foot practically pointing to my dick. She's still gorgeous and attractive, but she doesn't hold the pull for me she once did.

That doesn't mean I don't always want the upper hand. I do. It also means I can't seem to turn off my instinct to charm.

I sit down in the chair closest to her and kiss her on each cheek. "Ah, there's the love of my night." What the fuck am I saying? She's not the love of my night. Being a player is ingrained in my personality.

Luckily, Mariette sees right through my autopilot flirting and ignores the comment.

"So, I heard you set New York City on fire."

Huh? What does she know?

"What?" Jesus, please let her be messing with me.

"You and Miss Awkward. I got word you were brilliant and the New York companies are trying to co-opt my ballet."

I exhale.

"How did you know?"

"Come on, Max. You know all the artistic directors talk. Actually, Peter called me."

"Madsen?"

"Of course, Madsen. We've known each other a very long time. I'd venture to say he was one of Jerome's best friends."

An involuntary growl escapes my chest. "He was very taken with Miss Awkward."

"Is that a problem, Max?"

Fuck, I'm not doing this. I'm fucking coming out with it. "We need to talk about the bet."

"Ah, the bet. Yes, yes, I can guess what you're going to say. 'Mariette, it's over at the end of the week, and we might as well get an expensive suite at The Peninsula and fuck six ways to Sunday.' I thought you might say that. It's why I ordered the pizza and beer."

I place my elbows on the table with my head in my hands and cover my face. "No. That's not it at all."

Mariette moves closer. She takes both hands from my face and holds them gently, like a mom would do. "What's going on with you?

I shake my head, a tear that I had no idea was forming drops on the tabletop and all I can get out in a choked voice is, "I do owe you... pizza... and beer..."

"But no sex?" Mariette interrupts.

"You're in love."

"I'm in love."

We simultaneously murmur, blending our words together.

I can't stop the fucking tears and smile from coming, and I'm sure I've lost my mind. This three-sixty rollercoaster loop of emotions alone is scaring me about love—the feeling is crazy. It's too intense.

Mariette moves closer, brings her face close to mine and gives me a small, sweet kiss on the lips. Probably Mariette's idea of a consolation prize for losing.

She grins. "Finally!"

Finally? Finally what?

A shadow darkens the table, and I realize we're not alone. The waiter must be here. I look up from our intimate moment but am horrified to see it's not the waiter.

It's Victoria. A look of sheer disbelief on the face I adore. She looks at me and then fixes her gaze on Mariette.

"Mom, what's going on?"

Mom?

Mariette stands quickly, knocking over her chair and garnering the attention of every patron in Gino's.

"Victoria?" Why is she here, and why Mariette is so upset?

Mariette whispers loudly, "Oh, shit! Fleur!"

146

Very un-Mariette talk.

It's my turn to look at the two women suspiciously.

"Fleur? Victoria… is Fleur?"

Victoria says nothing, but her eyes well up.

Mariette gestures wildly—again, uncharacteristically. "Yes, she's Fleur. Fleur-de-Lis." She tries to put an arm around Miss Awkward, but Victoria flinches away.

Fleur-de-Lis? A visual of Victoria's fleur-de-lis tattoo enters my mind. My brain can't catch up. *What the…?*

"Fleur, it's not…" Mariette pleads. "It was a bet."

"A bet?" Victoria's voice is high and shrill.

"Yes, I bet Max he would fall in love in three months."

"And if he didn't?"

"Then he would buy me beer and pizza…"

Victoria tear-filled eyes bore into my soul. "That's it?"

Mariette drops the bombshell. "And I would sleep with him."

This is NOT FUCKING HAPPENING!

Victoria's eyebrows knit together, her eyes narrow and her lips thin out. "Well, congratulations, Mr. Thanks-A-Million. Looks like you won."

"Yes, I did." My meaning was 'Yes, I fell in love with you. I won,' but it didn't come out right

147

in context.

Victoria's expression changes from anger to dismay, and loud sobs jump from way down deep in her chest and rattle the air like bombs exploding.

"I mean no, I lost, but—" I'm completely fucking this up.

Livid, I round on Mariette, pointing a thumb in Victoria's direction. "She's your daughter?"

Mariette is now red-faced and tearful. "Yes!"

I swing back around to confront Victoria. "You're…?" But I don't finish as I catch sight of the heel of her black Converse and her shining ponytail disappearing out the door before she jumps on Mikhail and rockets north on Dearborn.

I run from Gino's, bellowing her name, trying to get her to stop like a crazed Marlon Brando in *A Streetcar Named Desire*. The only thing missing is a massive downpour of rain. *Fuck*! This could be a problem. She's gone. I run my hands through my hair in frustration and roar the only word that seems appropriate to the situation, "FUUUUUCK!"

People on the street hiss and scold me.

I'm not the only one screaming.

Mariette is out on the street, too, shrieking, "Fleur, Fleur come back!"

I've never known this woman to panic, but right now, I couldn't care less about her emotional stability.

Mariette grabs my upper arm, and I round on

her, my voice deep and agitated. "Mariette, what the fuck are you up to? What just happened?"

"Max, Fleur… Victoria *is* Fleur. My daughter."

"I thought your kid was like nine or ten. The pictures… in your office."

"They're old pictures, Max."

"So you weren't just dance partners. You had a kid with Jerome Ward. Jesus!"

"Yes, Victoria Awkward is my daughter with Jerome Ward. Please we have to stop her."

"That's why Madsen was so familiar with her?"

"Yes, Peter is Fleur's—I mean, Victoria's—godfather."

"Jesus! This is. So. Completely. Messed up." I point at Mariette. "You have so much explaining to do, but frankly, I'm more concerned with Victoria… Fleur… whoever the hell she is. What does she know?"

"Nothing, about us, about the bet. Until now. Max, I did all this for a reason. Kept her secret for a reason. Forbid you to pursue her. For a reason."

"What possible reason could you have to lie to me? To make her lie to me? I sure hope that's the case, that you made her, because I can't believe she'd do that without your influence."

"Yes, I told her not to tell you who she was."

I release a huge sigh. "Thank God. That excuses her behavior, but not yours."

"We need to go after her, Max!"

Getting right up in her face, the boxer in me coming out without restraint, I shout her down. "Mariette, I don't want to hear another word from you! I need to talk to Victoria. Now, do you think she went to the Waldorf?"

"I don't know, but it's probably the first place we should look. Let's go!"

"No! You are not coming. I need to talk to her alone. She's got the wrong idea, and I need to fix it. Give me your house keys."

"Max, no."

"Mariette, I'm not in the mood to argue. Give. Me. Your. Keys."

She reaches into her purse, fishes them out and slaps them into my hand. "Just let me know how she is, where she is."

I don't respond or offer any reassurance. Fucking Mariette. I can't contain how hugely pissed I am with her. I can't stand to look at her one more moment, so I leave her bawling her fucking eyes out on the corner of Dearborn and Congress. This is a disaster.

———————

I can't find Victoria anywhere. Every time I call her cell phone, it goes to voice mail. The texts I sent don't even indicate they've been received.

I'm worried she's turned off her phone.

The doorman at the Waldorf said she pulled up, ran in, ran out with a backpack and then took off on her bike.

The only logical places I think she'd go to are Gallant or her grandparent's house. I doubt she'd go to the studio—too obvious. *Dammit*! Her grandparents? Do they know about this jacked-up situation, too? I'm probably the only fool left in the dark about Victoria Awkward's true identity.

During the half hour drive to Oak Brook, I replay every interaction we've had since the moment I mentioned her ridiculous last name at the audition a few months ago. I also acknowledge the emotions I'm most familiar with—disappointment and betrayal. They're fighting it out with my love for her right now. It must be love that's driving me to find her. I never would have wasted my attentions on any human being in this manner before she stole my heart. And what must all this look like to her? Me with Mariette. So close. Mariette kissing me and whispering *finally*.

Finally? What the hell was that about?

———

The door to the Awkward's mansion opens before I even knock. Jerome and Kandis are there and usher me in immediately.

"I'm looking for Victoria."

Kandis loops her arm through mine and leads me to the sitting room off the foyer. "We know, dear. Mariette called us. She told us everything. We are so disappointed in her. Please believe we had no idea you didn't know she was Victoria's mother."

Victoria's grandparents both offer me a seat, but I refuse and pace frantically across the gigantic Oriental rug. "Is she here?"

"No, dear. We're both trying to figure out where she could have gone."

I want to punch something, and I'm feeling hemmed in being in this fancy room full of expensive furniture and fragile china knickknacky shit. Thank God Kandis has the sense to direct me toward the sofa in the middle of the room and make me sit.

They settle down on either side of me and speak in low, calm voices. I can feel my anxiety lessen. *How are they doing that?* Apart from Victoria, nobody has ever made me feel safe like this.

Vic's grandfather sighs. "Max, you need to know. Jerome Ward was my son, Jerome Awkward Jr. As you're aware, he was the *premier danseur* at the New York City Ballet."

I nod with my mouth agape. It's true. Jerome Ward is Victoria's father.

"He changed his name professionally. I'm

proud of our family name, but I have to admit Awkward is not a great name for a dancer." Jerome Sr. shakes his head and chuckles.

I feel a small internal, but worthless, victory. At least Victoria's grandfather and father both had some sense about that ridiculousness of that name for a dancer.

"Jerome was a big deal, probably could have been a superstar. Like really hit it big," Kandis adds proudly. "Mariette Gallant was his dance partner."

I already know all this, but I let her continue.

"And the love of his life."

That I was not aware of.

"They were secretly married and had Victoria. We all kept their marriage under wraps, at first for their profession and then for the protection of the baby."

They were married. "Why all the secrecy?" *Why wouldn't they tell the world*?

"They didn't want the company to know they were together. That sort of thing was frowned on back then, even more than today. They wanted Victoria to have a normal life, well… as normal as it can be when you're an heiress and the daughter of dancers. So, she lived in Brooklyn with Mariette and Jerome until they decided to move back here. They wanted to raise her near family, and we were it since Mariette's parents were deceased. Jerome and Mariette were just getting Gallant off the ground. They were going to launch the company and then announce their marriage and Victoria to the dance world."

"And then he died?"

"Yes, right before. Motorcycle accident."

Motorcycle. Victoria and that damn vintage motorcycle. It's all coming into focus now. "Was he riding Mikhail?

"No, one of his other bikes, but that's why Fleur is so fond of Mikhail," Mariette says, her voice piercing the bubble of our conversation.

We all turn and look at her.

Her normally calm countenance is screwed up, and she is blotchy and red-faced from crying.

On the tail end of a sob, she adds, "And why I panicked when I saw her drive off."

I stand and face Mariette. I'm still not happy with her. She may have ruined things with Victoria and me forever with her lies, but I'm starting to understand. I'm not the only person with a fucked-up past. Mariette has it in spades, and Victoria has inherited it.

"I'm so sorry, Max. So, so sorry. We have to find her."

"No, I have to find her. I have to talk to her first."

"She was always a private child like her father. She's probably gone somewhere she can think. Somewhere that makes her calm and happy," Jerome offers. "Where do you go when you're

154

unhappy or need to get away, Max?"

The happiest place I've ever been is New York, less than twenty-four hours ago with Victoria in my arms. She told me about the place she was happiest. Her happy place. What an odd coincidence he'd ask me that question in that way.

And it all begins to make sense. I have an idea.

I turn to Kandis. "I think I know where she is."

"Where?"

"She told me about a house by the ocean. She said you"—I point to Mariette—"and her father would take her there and she'd dance—"

Mariette finishes, "—in the kitchen with us. She's going to the cottage in the Hamptons. It's the only place I can think of."

Chapter 17

Not a New York State of Mind

Jerome, Kandis and Mariette all agree that the cottage in the Hamptons is where Victoria is headed.

Before I have a chance to say anything, Jerome is on the phone and Kandis is shoving Mariette and me out the door and down to a waiting black SUV with darkened windows.

"What's going on, Mr. Awkward?"

"You need to go get her, Max. You and Mariette. The both of you have hurt that girl and you need to fix it. For all of your sakes."

I grumble, "I don't need Mariette."

Mariette pushes past me and into the SUV. "I'm going, and you can't stop me."

Jerome Awkward holds his hand out, palm up, toward to the open car door. "Get in the car, Max. The AWK jet is being prepped, and the pilot has been called. Our car will take you to Chicago Executive Airfield. You don't have time to deal with a commercial flight."

I get in grudgingly. I'll go there with Mariette, but I don't have to fucking talk to her. As we drive north, I direct my attention out the window and watch as the angry Midwestern sky clouds over.

Clouded over. That's a good way to summarize this day. A beautiful day full of lightness and potential clouded over by stupidity. And not just Mariette's.

My own.

And maybe some of Victoria's, too. There's more than one victim in this misunderstanding.

————————

Two hours is a long time to not talk to someone when you're trapped in a fancy tin can hurtling through the sky. It would have been worse on a regular flight, sitting right next to her the whole way. Being on the private jet makes it bearable, at least.

Mariette is on the opposite side of the plane in a grouping of seats facing each other. I am in a similar grouping on the other side, and we have our backs to each other.

Even this far away, I want to wring her neck while simultaneously wondering what this whole fucking deception was about.

I stick my earphones in and open the music app on my phone. Navigating to the playlist, I scroll to find something to help me gather my thoughts on what to say to Victoria. To find the right words to tell her I'm sorry and that nothing happened with her mom. Fuck her mom! It's so messed up to think of Mariette that way.

I don't scroll far when the title of a playlist grabs me: Awkward 80s Mix (and some other stuff). Victoria must have put it on my phone sometime during our trip to New York.

I've heard her sing every one of these songs in the time since we met. Sometimes, horrible pitchy versions while she wore her headphones. The thought makes me smile. Probably the first smile to cross my lips since looking into her pained eyes at Gino's. When I mull it over, I've laughed and smiled more since I've known her than in all the twenty-six years before. All my smiles belong to her.

Then Michael Jackson's voice registers in my brain, and the lyrics to "She's Out of My Life" become far too real and painful. His halting words and the audible tears in the final notes squeeze my heart.

The attendant taps me on the shoulder. I scrub my wet eyes with the heels of my palms and swallow a few times. When I remove my earphones, she quietly announces our descent into Long Island MacArthur Airport. This journey is much different from my last two flights in and out of New York City. No lines, no security and, most notably, no Victoria.

I'm pulling myself together when Mariette plops—as much as a ballerina can even do so—in the seat directly in front of me. I've avoided her for the entire flight and now she approaches me?

"What?"

"So, you're in love with my daughter? With Fleur?"

"I'm in love with a gorgeous, amazing woman named Victoria Awkward. Her being your daughter has nothing to do with it."

"Good." With that she returns to her seat across the aisle and puts on her seatbelt.

Good? What the fuck have I gotten myself into?

————————

We're met at the foot of the plane by Tommy, the limousine driver who was on call for Victoria and me all last weekend. He smiles and tilts his head a bit.

"Hello, Ms. Gallant. And welcome back, Mr. Devereaux." Evidently, he works for AWK. Shit! Everybody in the whole universe knows everything except me!

Mariette shakes Tommy's hand. "Thank you for coming all the way out here from the city, Tommy."

"Hey, you're the boss, applesauce."

Mariette giggles like a small girl. "I've really missed you, Tommy."

Even Tommy-the-fucking-limo-driver knows who Mariette and Vic really are.

"I'm guessing you're going to the Amagansett house, Ms. Gallant?"

"Yes, we think Fleur may have gone there. She's... she's rather upset with us. Me, really, I think."

I want to punch someone, anyone. I can't help feeling I've been played, which is a shitty feeling for a player. To top it all off, Mariette is starting to make me feel bad, dammit. I still don't understand why all the secrecy, but I'm riding out this drama because I'm interested in finding out.

———————

Thank God, it's dark in the limo and outside because I spend the entire trip up the coast clenching and unclenching my fists, punching my palm and answering Tommy's questions with terse, one-word replies. I usually temper any anxiety with dancing, boxing or banging. Though I'm not particularly proud of that last option anymore, I'm not used to having to exert so much mental energy managing my emotions. I just want to fucking get there, already. Get to Victoria. I'm not even positive she's there, but it's my only hope.

Eventually we pull up to a gray shake-shingled house with white trim. The sun is just about to set, but the cottage is lit up with exterior lighting. *This is the cottage*? It's big enough for my entire family back in Dorchester and several of my aunts, uncles and loudmouthed cousins.

I don't know who exited the limo faster, Mariette or me. We walk side by side up to the house.

Once on the porch, Mariette suddenly stops and turns back to Tommy, who has gotten out and is coming around to the passenger side even though there's nobody to let out.

"Tommy, can you wait?"

"No problem, boss. I'm at your service."

"I don't know how long this will be."

"Again, no problem, Ms. Gallant."

All the lights on the lower level are blazing. A good sign. The door is unlocked when I try it. I don't know what to do, so I just step in. The foyer has bright white walls and dark wooden floors. I instantly smell the ocean and something else. Her. Victoria's scent.

"She's here. I know it," I whisper to myself.

161

Mariette and I both begin calling.

"Fleur?"

"Vic? Are you here, baby?"

We divide and move through opposite parts of the first floor, and when we meet again in the kitchen, I notice the large French doors to the back of the house are open. A sea breeze blows the sheer white drapes into the great room.

The glow from the sun almost completely gone, but I see a light far down on the beach.

"Mariette?" I speak my first civil word to her. "Do you think that's her on the beach? Alone?"

Mariette opens her mouth, but before any words escape, Victoria appears between the flowing curtains, her eyes red and her hair tousled and unkempt. "No, I'm right here."

Even completely wrecked, my darling girl is gorgeous. I want to wrap her in my arms and make everything right. I move toward her, but she puts up both hands, palms facing me, to stop my approach.

"Max? Why are you here? Why are either of you here? Shouldn't you be somewhere laughing it up about how "Fleur the Fool" fell for Maximilian "Thanks-A-million" Devereaux?"

"It's not like that, Victoria." My voice sounds tight and false, even to me.

"And you, Mom, shouldn't you be trying to get him in bed. I mean, come on, that has to be why you didn't want me anywhere near him. Don't worry, guys. I've got it all figured out."

"No, Fleur, darling. It's not like that at all. I had an idea, and it all went horribly wrong. You misunderstand."

"What's to misunderstand about you kissing the man I—" She doesn't finish. She just swallows several times and chokes back a squeaking noise.

What was she about to say?

"And him, looking deeply into your eyes."

I must interject. "I wasn't looking deeply into her eyes. I was getting ready to tell her about you." I approach Victoria again, but she glides quickly all the way across the room, shaking her head.

Mariette advances on her slowly as I back away. It's like trying to calm a skittish, wounded animal in the wild.

Mariette's voice gets lower as she takes small steps toward my beautiful, anguished girl. "Please, let me explain. This isn't Max's fault. It's all on me." Mariette's final words are hitched and thick with tears.

"Fine." Victoria crumples onto a low ottoman. "I'm too exhausted to fight."

Chapter 18

Meeting Fleur

Mariette kneels slowly in front Victoria. She doesn't reach out for her. She doesn't look her in the eye. She assumes a position of deference, of subservience, of one pleading for forgiveness.

"I'm sorry. I'm so sorry you saw Max and me like that at Gino's. I can see why you'd think we were together. That we were deceiving you. But, sweetie, he wasn't. And even though I made a bad decision about something, I wasn't trying to embarrass you or hurt you."

Victoria looks up at me, and I try with all my might to communicate that what Mariette is saying is true—or at least I think it is. I nod my agreement because even though I don't know where Mariette is going with all of this, I need Victoria to know we didn't mean to hurt her and I'm sorry.

Mariette looks up long enough to see Victoria and me exchange confused stares.

"I love you, Fleur. I love you so much. Your

daddy loved you so, so much. I want you to be as happy as I was with your dad." Mariette reaches up and squeezes the top of Victoria's closed hand. Then Mariette looks up at me.

"And Max." She stands and walks over to me. "Whether you know it or not, you were lost, sad. It was killing me watching you go from meaningless hookup to meaningless hookup. Especially when I knew the perfect person, the perfect counter to you."

"Victoria?" I ask, already sure that I've guessed correctly. "That's why you said, 'Finally.' "

"Yes, finally, you found the one, Max," Mariette whispers loud enough for Victoria to hear. "I took a risk choosing you for my daughter. I know your past, but I also know you're a good man with a good heart. You've just been lost. You needed the right person to find you. To see you. I was always watching. Monitoring." Mariette doesn't look at Fleur, she keeps her eyes on me, but she raises her voice a bit more to say, "Fleur, I know you're a smart girl. I knew you'd see the good in Max."

Vic has finally tuned in. Mariette takes my hand and leads me over to Victoria, who stands as I approach. Vic and I are finally face-to-face with Mariette holding one of each of our hands. "Max, Fleur, if I'd tried to introduce you two, it never would have worked. You are both so stubborn. So, when you proposed it, I played along with your silly bet, Max. It was my backward, though poorly executed, way of getting you to meet each other."

"And, Victoria, I made that deal with you, allowing you to audition. I didn't want any of the dancers or you, Max, to give her special treatment, so I asked her to keep her identity quiet. Then all I had to do was forbid you both from getting involved with each other, and you took it from there."

So much that didn't make sense now does.

"The easiest way to make me want to do something…," I whisper.

"…is to tell me not to," Victoria finishes my sentence.

Looking at Victoria but talking to Mariette, I say, "You know us pretty well. Mariette? Can Victoria and I have a few minutes?"

Mariette takes Victoria's hand and puts in in mine. "Max, I'd like you to meet Victoria "Fleur-de-Lis" Awkward, my daughter with Jerome Awkward. Of course, you can have a few minutes. You can have more than a few minutes."

She turns and walks toward the front door.

Victoria looks at me and then puts one finger up to give her a minute. She releases my hand and chases after Mariette.

"Mom?" When she reaches Mariette, Victoria pulls her closer to the door out of earshot, and for a moment I think she's going to throw her out.

166

They appear tense, but then Victoria smiles, and it's soon mirrored by Mariette.

Mariette whispers something in Vic's ear. Then, while waving over her shoulder, she intentionally loudly declares, "I'm going to have Tommy take me into the city. I have a few people to catch up with. And you two need some time alone."

"But what about rehearsal?" I ask. We're supposed to begin rehearsing the show tomorrow.

"I'll call Rachel and tell her to start rehearsing the corps tomorrow. Fleur can start the day after."

Chapter 19

One More Night

Victoria stands in the foyer and watches her mother walk out to Tommy and the waiting limo. I'm still trying to come to grips with the realization that Mariette is Victoria's mother and Victoria is Fleur.

Before she turns around and I must look in her eyes, I whisper just loud enough to carry across the distance between us, "Go for a walk on the beach with me."

She almost pirouettes in place as she turns. Her shoulders are slumped and her eyes puffy from tears. "A walk? Aren't you exhausted? I'm exhausted."

"Just a short one down to the water." I extend my hand to her, but she doesn't move toward me. I drop my hand to my side in defeat. "Is there a flashlight anywhere?"

Finally, Victoria moves, and I thank God it's toward me and not away. Our eyes only meet briefly. She raises her chin in the direction of the kitchen. "On the counter. Just there."

On the beach, we walk in silence close enough that our hands and wrists eventually brush. I can't stand not knowing what she's thinking, and I have so much to say to her, to ask her. I take her hand, and to my amazement, she doesn't pull away. We walk a little farther before everything I want to tell her comes to me, and I stop. This pulls her back a little, and she spins around to finally look me square in the eye.

"We only have tonight, Victoria."

"Max. It's—"

"Just hold on. Victoria. I'm a scumbag. Some would say a manwhore. There's a totally screwed-up reason why, but it's not nearly good enough. A reason why *I'm* not good enough. For you."

"Call me Fleur."

"Really, that's all you have to say about what I just said?"

"No, there's more. Call me Fleur. But only all the time and only in front of everyone."

My exhausted, rumpled, gorgeous, poised love makes a joke in the middle of a tense apology." I laugh aloud to the moon.

"Fleur-de-Lis. Fleur. It fits you." I think back to the plane ride. I Googled the meaning of Fleur-de-Lis. "Life, Light and Perfection"

Victoria lets out a harsh sarcastic laugh of distain. "Hardly."

"Let me finish. I'm a womanizer. I know that

169

about myself. Mariette saw something more, I guess."

"She saw what I see. A man with a heart full of love but nobody in his life to really give it to."

"You figured me out. A lot faster than I did. It took eight years and you coming into my world."

"I shouldn't have lied to you about who I really was. I shouldn't have listened to my mother."

"I should be angry with you for you not telling me who you are, but you know what? I can't be. Somehow, you seem like more of a victim in this manipulation than I do. Why didn't you tell me Jerome Ward was your dad?"

"I was about to. A lot of times in New York. I was going to tell Mom how I felt about you when we got home, but when I got to the Waldorf, the housekeeper told me she'd gone to Gino's East, so I thought I'd surprise her. Then I saw you two—together—looking so close. Some surprise! I was so confused. It hurt to see you with her. And the bet? I never thought you or she would do something like that. I was so hurt. And angry."

"You can blame me for the bet. It was my stupid idea. Your mom—man, that feels weird—went into it with better intentions than I did. Intentions for both of us."

Victoria inhales sharply and squeezes my hand. A strangled cry escapes, and she turns her face away from me and looks at the water.

I wish she would look at me. The only thing

giving me hope is that she's still holding my hand.

"It doesn't change how I felt, but I understand."

"Vic—dammit, it may take me a while to get used to this. Fleur, I've only seen you angry one other time. When you first started at Gallant. When I didn't know how to deal with how I felt around you. When you didn't know why I was treating you badly."

Finally she turns her face completely toward mine. "I was angrier than that. I didn't even want to throw my dance bag. All I wanted to do was run."

She moves in and kisses me softly and quickly on the lips before she releases my hand and runs toward the cottage.

"Vic—I mean, Fleur!" I shout with a hoarse voice while scrambling after her. I catch up with her right before she reaches the stairs to the deck.

"Don't... Don't run away from me. Ever again."

"I wasn't running away just now."

"No? It sure looked like running."

"No, I was enticing. I don't want to talk anymore. I just want to be with you. And not on the beach. Don't you know? I love you, Max."

"You do? Even after all this craziness?"

"Yes, I love you so much."

"Fleur, baby, I love you. I love you to distraction. I can't breathe. I can't sleep. God, I

171

sound like that Robert Palmer song. And that's another thing—80s music. It's freaking everywhere these days." I reach in my pocket, pull out my phone and hold it up.

"I guess you found the playlist I made for you."

Chapter 20

Addicted to Love

I reach down, place my hands at the back of Fleur's knees and scoop her into my arms. She wraps her arms around my neck just like we're rehearsing part of *Desperately Seeking Susan*. The part where Dez takes Roberta home. I carry her upstairs. She's sighs, her body relaxes and her breathing evens out. Her warm, sweet breath on my neck calms me like nothing before. She's no longer running. She's here.

Fleur helps me navigates. "When you get to the top of the stairs, turn left and go through the double doors."

I kick the doors, and they open together to reveal a huge master bedroom, all white and cream with a large dark-cherry stained bed to my right. Moonlight reflects off the ocean and streams in through the three large cathedral windows facing the beach. I scan the room once, but am distinctly aware of Fleur yawning into the crook of my neck.

It may be inappropriate, given the amount of

talking we still very much need to do, but I feel myself stiffen with desire.

I walk to the bed and place Fleur on the floor next to it while keeping my arms around her.

Looking down into the face of the one I love, I say, "I'm so sorry. Today started out as the best day of my life, then it became the worst and now…"

Fleur sighs, then reaches up and wipes away a single tear from my cheek with her sweet, delicate fingers. A tear I didn't even know was there. She places her fingers in her mouth and tastes my tear. With a smile that lights up my world as much as the moonlight lights up the room, she says, "And now, it's perfect."

"But we—"

Fleur moves her face close to mine but does touch me. "I'm tired of talking. And crying. You love me. That's all that matters."

I drag my lips ever so slowly and barely across her forehead. "I want to make love to you. To Fleur." Then I move my lips across her cheeks and nose. Just feeling her, not kissing. She shivers. "Is that okay? You're not too tired?"

"I'm a mess." Fleur gently glides her lips across my cheek near the corner of my lip, mimicking my touch. "But no, I'm not too tired."

I finally kiss her. Soft, sweet, barely there pressure. She opens her lips minutely and then wider, and suddenly, we can't kiss each other enough. I pick her up again for just a moment before placing her on the bed. Her hair fans out across the pillows.

Just like our last time in a bed, she pulls me down to her. I take my time, kissing every inch of skin on her face and neck and shoulders before peeling off her tank top and bra. I take her awe-inspiring, pert, not-too-big breasts in my hands. Fleur arches into them and runs her hands through my hair. She pulls me closer and kisses me like she's trying to bring me back to life, which she needn't do because she already has by loving me.

I slide my hand down her flat, muscular stomach, across her slim hips and around to her lower back and pull her closer.

We touch, kiss and slowly remove any pesky garments, dropping each one off the side of the bed.

When we're finally naked, she pushes her pelvis up and slides her body down until my shaft is lined up where we both want it to be. "Please, Max, I need you. I need you in me now."

Who am I to refuse my life, light and perfection? I slide into her with purpose.

"Ooh," she moans with each gained centimeter. Once I'm seated in her warmth, we still for a moment and just fall into each other's gaze.

This is the moment.

"Come home to me. Come home *with* me,

Fleur."

"Why are you asking like that? Now?"

"I don't know. It's just… home is where you can be your worst self, but when I'm with you, I'm home and I'm my best self. I love you. Come home with me."

Fleur smiles. "You are home."

She takes me further in, if that's even possible, and begins rocking into me, and I thrust to meet her every movement. I cannot hold on much longer, but I won't finish without her. When she groans loudly and I feel her clench around me, it's only then I let go. My world spins and my vision blurs and I think I might pass out.

When I regain my focus seconds later, I look down at the most beautiful thing in my world.

Miss Awkward.

Victoria.

Fleur.

Home.

Chapter 21

It's in His Kiss

I wake in a state of confusion. It only takes moments to recall the past twenty-four hours. New York to Chicago and back. The emotional day and night of discovery and redemption.

My phone and my girl are gone. The old flip digital alarm clock next to bed clicks over: 7:37. Another thing from Fleur's beloved 80s.

I'm on the edge of panic that Fleur isn't still in bed with me when I hear music downstairs.

I throw on my jeans and walk down the stairs stealthily. Partway down the first flight, I can hear "The Shoop Shoop Song." When I turn the corner on the landing and start down the second flight, I can see past the expansive kitchen. There's movement through the open French doors out on the deck

There she is. My Fleur. In nothing but my gray T-shirt and panties, barefoot and performing the ending and curtain call of *Desperately Seeking*

Susan.

There's only one problem. This isn't a solo. She should have a partner. I pad down the remaining steps and glide out to where she is.

She's facing away from me.

When I place my hands on her hips and lift her during a section where a lift occurs, she gasps in surprise.

"Max," she whispers while suspended above me. Her voice, delighted and content, sends a jolt of electricity through me.

I slide her down my body as the choreography dictates. "I'm right here, Fleur."

"I didn't mean to wake you. I bugged out of Chicago without my headphones."

Her 'bugged out' comment causes a momentary internal wince of guilt. I do my best to ignore it. "Well, apart from the initial shock of you and my phone missing, this is my second favorite way to wake up."

I scoop my phone off the table on the deck while I dance and maneuver Fleur into the kitchen. The music changes to Carly Simon singing "You Belong to Me." Perfect. I take her in my arms to slow down.

Fleur's eyes well up. "We're dancing." Her voice cracks.

"Yes."

"In the kitchen."

"Uh-huh," I reply in a soft low growl into her

ear.

"Did you plan this?"

"I'd like to think I'm that smooth, but the idea only came to me after I saw you dancing on the deck and joined you."

"You have good instincts."

"Not always. My instincts have primarily been about my own selfish desires. It's so strange to think of someone else first. Strange and freeing."

"Thank you."

"For what?"

"Being you. Making that bet."

I stop and step away from her to gauge her expression. It's nothing but sincere. I'm sure my face is a giant question mark. "Seriously?"

"Yes, and for loving me enough to come find me."

I pull her back into my embrace and kiss her hair and forehead. "That wasn't even an option. You're the one, Fleur. You're my forever *pas de deux*."

She sighs and then tilts her face up to mine to leave a trail of tiny, tickly kisses across my jawline. I'm wholly unprepared for what she says next.

"I'm hungry. Can you cook?" She knows just the way to keep me on my toes.

"Yes, I make pretty good omelets. Uh, before we make breakfast, I want to ask you… uh, let me say it another way." Here goes. "I can think of a

179

great way to get rid of that Awkward name. Change it to Devereaux. Even your dad changed his name," I blurt out like a guy asking a girl out to the movies for the first time. All my "playerness" is gone.

"Max, we've talked about this."

"I'm not being clear enough. Fleur,"—taking one of her hands, I drop to one knee in the kitchen of the place where she's happiest—"marry me."

Fleur's eyes well up, and each spills a single tear. "Oh!" She covers her mouth with her free hand and looks at the ceiling as she blinks away the tears.

"Stand up, Max."

I do as I'm commanded.

Fleur wipes away any remaining tears with the back of her hands. Then she pushes onto her tiptoes, takes my face in both hands and kisses me. Not a sweet thank you kiss, but full, open kiss with lips begging to be kissed back. I willing do. Our tongues lave one another. Surely, she is saying yes.

Fleur pulls away, and I need to catch my breath from the overwhelming passion she put into that *baiser Francais*.

"Max Devereaux, I will say yes to that… someday."

Not the answer I wanted. I'm about to protest when Fleur puts a finger up to my open lips.

"I promise, but first I need to do something. And I need you to do something." She picks up my

180

phone from the counter and punches in some numbers. *What the hell*? How did this spontaneous proposal turn, well, awkward?

"No, Mom, it's not Max. Yes, we're fine." Fleur looks at me and winks. "Yes, yes, we'll be ready to go in an hour or so. I want to discuss something on the plane. I think we need to do something. Okay, okay see you then."

Chapter 22

Sweet Home, Chicago

On the AWK jet back to Chicago, I sit alone in the grouping of seats away from Mariette and Fleur. They've had their heads together for a long time. They both look concerned, but after more tears and a few gulping smiles, they hug. I can't hear what they're saying, but from the looks of the interaction, I think they've talked things through and forgiven one another. Watching them together and their shared mannerisms, I wonder how I didn't see it earlier. Fleur is clearly Mariette's child.

Mariette picks up her phone and places a call. I'm so exhausted from the storm of misunderstanding I allow myself to close my eyes.

I must have fallen asleep because I wake to Mariette's voice.

"My darling Fleur-de-Lis. It's so bizarre watching you become fully formed when I'm still working on myself."

"Mother, you are my inspiration. You are my

role model for life. You and Father and Grandma and Grandpa…"

"And Max?"

"Yes, and now Max."

I can't pretend to be asleep any longer, so I open my eyes and find Fleur and Mariette standing beside me, holding hands and looking down at me. Two gorgeous women. Perhaps the two most important women in my life.

"Talking about me?"

Fleur answers with a giggle, "As a matter of fact, we were."

Mariette motions for Fleur to take the seat beside me.

"She's all yours, Max. See that she gets some sleep the rest of the way back. Rehearsal tonight, you know. And a big day tomorrow."

Mariette Gallant may be Fleur's mother, but she is still the artistic director of Gallant Ballet.

"Will do, boss."

"Why is it a big day tomorrow?"

"I'll tell you tonight at rehearsal."

Mariette returns to her section at the front of the cabin and takes a window seat with her back to us.

I grab a blanket, and after tucking Fleur under my arm so her head is against my chest, I cover her and say, "Sleep. Boss's orders."

I feel her lips pout against my pec. "Really, you don't want to fool around? Join the mile high club, maybe?"

Again, she shocks me. "Tempting, but not with your mother on the plane."

"Boo."

"Another time, my light, another time."

Eventually after some heavy sighs, she sleeps.

Fleur and I stand in Mariette's office, preparing ourselves. Fleur is dressed in a blue wrap dress with a deep V neck. The color makes her strawberry blonde hair, which has been released from its almost constant bun or braid, look fierier. It cascades in soft waves past her shoulders to curl right above the tops of her breasts.

"Are you ready for this?"

After a few swallows, Fleur whispers, "I think so."

Mariette comes in to get us, sophisticated and poised in a white sheath dress.

"It's time, darling. Let's do this."

After Fleur's first rehearsal last night, Mariette announced to the company that there would be no morning class. Instead, there was to be a press conference in the main studio. Evidently, Mariette had contacted Gallant's business manager, Theresa. She arranged the press conference. The interview was scheduled with the local Chicago news stations, but when hints were given about what was going to be revealed, it was picked up by national news outlets E! News, the *New York Tribune*, *Dance Universe* and *En Pointe* magazine. Big day, indeed.

Mariette steps from the office, leaving the door open so we can stand just inside it and watch. Jerome Sr. and Kandis are on the other side of the room. They're smiling, and I imagine they are as scared and excited as the rest of us are.

There are camera flashes and some loud whispers.

"There she is…"

"I wonder if the rumors are true."

Mariette waves royally at the crowd of media and sits in front of one of the two microphones. After taking a moment, she begins.

"Good Morning, I'm Mariette Gallant, artistic director of Gallant Ballet and Studios, here in Chicago. I'm so glad you could all join me today. I'm going to make a statement, and then I'll take questions."

The cameras continue clicking, the flashes fast and blinding.

Mariette is unfazed. She is also not using any notes whatsoever.

"Nineteen years ago, I was a dancing in New York at the City Ballet where I met my dance partner, Jerome Ward. Jerome's real name was

Jerome Awkward Jr. You're probably aware that Awkward is a well-known name in Chicago. His family owns AWK Steel. As you all know, Jerome tragically lost his life in a motorcycle accident very soon after Gallant Ballet opened. None of that is new information." Mariette's voice hitches on the last word.

The room gets quiet. No cameras flash, only the whirl of batteries and video cameras.

"What you don't know, what the world doesn't know, is that Jerome Ward was more than my dance partner... He, he, he was my life partner. He was my husband."

The crowd lets loose with soft audible gasps and a chorus of "*What*?"

"Jerome and I married secretly. Only his parents knew for the longest time. Then I became pregnant. We were over the moon. To protect our careers and our child, I took a sabbatical once I was starting to show, and our sweet girl was born. She is now grown into a beautiful woman and a beautiful dancer. Her father would be so proud. I know I am."

More gasps and rumbles from the group.

"Where is she, Mariette?"

"What's her name?"

"I'm so glad you asked." Mariette turns her face to the office door. "Victoria! Can you come out here?"

Fleur squeezes my hand. I pull her in for a

186

quick hug and kiss on the temple. "Welcome to the world, Victoria," I whisper.

She gives me the side eye and then walks to Mariette's side and sits in front of the second microphone. She holds her hand up to the side of her face to block the waves of flashes from the cameras.

"This is my daughter—Jerome Ward's daughter—Victoria Awkward. She's eighteen. She's recently joined the company at Gallant and has been cast in a major part in our first production of the season."

"Hello," Fleur says into the microphone.

Suddenly, more cameras flash. Members of the press call Victoria and Mariette's names and shout questions.

"Why did you keep your marriage secret?"

"Romances between partners are not really encouraged in the dance world. There's too much risk. A good pair can disintegrate on the dance floor if it doesn't work out. We were protecting our careers. We were going to reveal after Gallant Ballet was up and running, but then... we lost Jerome." Mariette takes Fleur's hand. "It was too hard to share the secret of our love with the world then."

"Victoria, how do you feel about your mother's decision to keep you a secret? How did you manage that all these years?"

Victoria scoots her chair closer to her mother

and wraps her other hand around their already clenched hands. She looks at Mariette, smiles a straight-line smile and squares her shoulders as she faces down the reporters.

"I have felt so many things about the way I was raised. And just like any child, I've been angry at my parents at times for decisions they've made about my life. But here's the truth. My truth. I was raised by parents who loved me. Who only thought of me. I was the child of a secret marriage, but I was also a child of privilege, an heiress. That put me at risk to be harmed, stolen or exploited. Did I appreciate that when I was nine and my father died and my mother wasn't around because she was building a business? No, I did not. But I do now because I was raised by her and my wonderful grandparents. I understand. I'm old enough to understand that people make choices that affect others and they don't realize it. They make decisions that they think will help or protect the people they love." She looks at Mariette, who slowly opens and closes her eyes and nods once. "Sometimes, those decisions go wrong and hurt the person they were meant to protect."

Victoria looks over at me. I step out of the doorway. The reporters pick up on her change of focus and *Pop*! *Pop*! *Pop*! The camera flashes catch me unaware.

Victoria continues, "And sometimes, those ill-conceived decisions go very, very right."

She's talking about me and Mariette and our stupid, thoughtless bet that turned into biggest, best payoff of all.

The crowd goes crazy with questions once again.

"Mariette!"

"Victoria!"

"Mariette, tell us about Victoria and the new season. How do the dancers in the company feel about your daughter dancing a lead role?"

Mariette tells them Victoria earned her role on her own merit. Nobody knew they were related, not even me, the choreographer.

Victoria and Mariette field a few more questions and finish the press conference by posing for pictures.

I usher them back into Mariette's office, and the three of us whoop with happiness. It's all out there. No more secrets.

For the second time in two days, I drop to my knee. This time in front of Mariette.

"Victoria Awkward, Fleur, I asked you yesterday and you said there was something you had to do. I'm guessing the press conference and Mariette acknowledging you was that thing. So, now will you marry me and change your name to mine?"

Again, she doesn't take me up on my proposal and suggestion. She says there is still something I have to do.

189

"I want to meet your family. I think you should reconnect with them."

"Fleur, that's a lot to ask."

"I know."

———————

I'm not angry about Fleur's refusal of my proposal—for a second time. I love her and I will try to do what she's asked, but I don't think I can do it yet.

In just two months, the former Miss Victoria Awkward will make her debut in Gallant Ballet's season opener, *La Sylphide*, as Victoria Ward.

I still have some work to do to make sure she has a last name that is more acceptable in my eyes. One that starts with a *D*.

Chapter 23

Wedding Vows

" . . . To have and to hold from this day forward, for better for worse, for richer, for poorer, in sickness and in health, to love and to cherish until you are parted by death. Do you make this solemn vow?" the minister asks.

"I do! Again," Jerome Sr. answers, sending the all the attendees into fits of laughter and applause.

What can I do but join them? No matter how I feel, I'm honored that the Awkwards invited me to their big fiftieth anniversary vow renewal and party. Jerome and Kandis are adorable dressed in their wedding clothes like they were in 1965. Fleur squeezes my hand. Maybe she knows I'm thinking about my two proposals and the fact that she's turned me down twice. Or maybe she's just enjoying seeing her grandparents so happy.

I know the ball is in my court. I need to do some reflecting and grow a pair. I'm just not there yet. I'm still too hurt and angry to jump right into a relationship with my parents.

After the ceremony, Fleur walks me around the grounds of her grandparent's estate. It's beautiful, but the only thing I want to do is look at her. We've had a helluva week: New York, the workshop, figuring out we're in love, the misunderstanding and the press conference. Between all that and rehearsals for the show, we haven't had much time to talk, let alone kiss or make love.

I stop under a tree and press her back up against it. I'm just about to kiss her when…

"Ahem!" A voice interrupts our impending lip-lock.

Fleur startles but then immediately relaxes when she realizes it's her grandfather. I pull away and turn to face him flushing like a little girl. Looks like we'll be waiting a bit longer. I'm not used to parents or grandparents cockblocking me.

"Hello, sir."

"Please, Max, call me Jerome. Or Jer. Whatever you like. You're almost family."

I roll my eyes at Fleur and then cock my head when I tell Jerome, "Yeah, not yet."

Fleur slaps me on the arm playfully.

"Victoria, may I borrow this guy for a minute? I think we have some talking to do."

"Sure, Grandpa. I'll just go see what Mom and Grandma are up to." Fleur flits out from under my arm and away from the tree. "See you in the tent. I think there's about fifteen minutes until dinner is served."

We both watch her as she moves across the lawn like the sylph she'll soon be portraying. When Jerome looks at me, I cast my eyes down and toe the grass in front of me. I wonder if I'm in trouble.

"Max?"

I straighten up and look Jerome in the face. He has a serious look in his eyes and his brows are furrowed. I've never seen this man anything but amiable, so I'm getting a bit concerned.

"Yes?"

"You know Victoria's father is gone. I'm really the only father figure she has, and as such, I was wondering if there was something you wanted to ask me?"

"I don't think so, sir." I'm completely confused. What would I possibly need to ask Jerome? It's not like I'm going to ask him for sex tips or money.

"Nothing? About you and my granddaughter?"

Then it hits me, and I feel like the biggest lunkhead at the Celtic Gym.

"Oh, about proposing?"

"Yes, Max."

"Okay, yes... You're right... I should have asked you first, sir. I get carried away around her."

Jerome laughs softly, "I've noticed."

I clear my throat to stop myself from blabbing on. "Jerome, may I have your blessing to marry your granddaughter, Victoria?"

Now Jerome is looking at the ground, toeing the earth and shaking his head.

"Welllll…"

Crap! He's going to say no.

"Kandis and I are very fond of you, Max. Did you know that?

"No, sir."

"Well, we are."

"Thank you, sir."

"You're welcome. And we can't think of a better person for our girl. Yes, of course you can marry her."

I breathe out a huge audible sigh of relief and put my hand up to lean against the tree for support. That conversation seemed as though it was going in a bad direction for a moment there.

I reach out with my other hand and shake Jerome's as he guffaws.

"Thank you, sir. You really had me going there."

"I was just messing with you, Max. Heck, it's going to be fun to have someone like a son around again." I detect a slight hitch in the old guy's voice. "You just gotta get that stuff with your family figured out first. I know my granddaughter, and she's stubborn as a mule."

"I think that's one of the things I like best about her, sir. She's beautiful and poised and talented and way too good for me, but her spirit, the part that makes her stubborn, is what my heart found so irresistible."

"Hell, Max. That's damn beautiful. Tell her that and she may forget about meeting your family."

"I doubt it, sir."

"Me, too." He chuckles again. "Oh, one more thing." Jerome reaches in his pocket and pulls out a box. A black velvet box. "This is a family heirloom. It was supposed to go to Jerome Jr. for Mariette, but when I offered, he turned it down. Told me to wait until everybody knew. That day never came. So I want you to take it, and the next time you try proposing to my granddaughter, you give her this. See if that doesn't help your cause."

I open the box and a good-sized rectangular diamond in an old fashioned setting sparkles before me.

I'm speechless. He's unlike any father or father figure I've known. "This ought to do it."

Jerome wipes away a few tears before slapping me on the back.

"She'd be a fool to say no again. Now, stuff that in your pocket. We've got a party to go to. I want to dance with my bride."

We walk side by side down to the tent.

"Great idea, sir."

"Max, just call me Jerome."

"Jerome." I reply.

Victoria's grandfather slaps me on the back. "Forget calling me Jerome, Max. Maybe just call me Grandpa."

Chapter 24

Call Me

Not long after Fleur told me that I needed to reach out and repair my relationship with my family before she'd agree to marry me, I began making phone calls surreptitiously. Oh, I stalled for a good month, even after my chat with Jerome. The idea of talking to my father was unbearable. To my mother, painful. My sisters, on the other hand? Yeah, I could start with them.

I haven't told Fleur about the calls. I want to make sure everything is cool with my family before I do.

So the calls started to Massachusetts—Dorchester—to my sisters, Janine, Colleen, Abby and Erika. At first, they were short, terse and weird, but little by little, it was soon like no time had passed at all. I was closest to Erika growing up; she's the one I followed to ballet. Janine, older than me by ten years, was my mother when Mom wasn't around. Colleen and Abby are my twin sisters. They've been tough DOT broads for as long as I've known them. They did their best to protect me from my dad, at least when I was little, but after a while, they couldn't. I had to do it myself. Every single one of them was thrilled to hear from me, and every single one of them has kept up with me by searching the internet for any news. Erika says she'd checked Facebook every day since I left to see if I've joined. That'll be the day! It's gotten to the point where I call at least one of them every day. We even have a group text message going.

The one thing we haven't discussed is our father.

When I talked to Janine last night, she told me I needed to call Mom. She didn't bring Dad into it, but I assumed she meant both. I rejected the idea right out of the box.

"I don't want to risk... ya know, *him* answering."

Janine grunted. "Ha! No chance of that."

"What d'ya mean?"

"Max, just call Ma. Call her. I promise, it's gonna be okay."

"Okay, 'Neen. If you say so."

"I say so," she replies and then proceeds to give me the phone number for my mother. I can't remember our old number, but this one doesn't seem familiar.

I wait one more day, and then I take the risk.

The line rings one, two, three times. I rashly make a deal with myself that if no one picks up by five, I'll hang up.

Four. Click.

"Hello?"

I guess this is happening.

Thank God, it's a woman's voice. A familiar voice, if not a little tired and maybe a little older.

"Mom? Ma?"

There's a sharp inhalation and then, "Max?"

"Yes, it's me."

"Really? Is it really you, Max?"

"Yeah, Ma, It's me." I hear crying on the other end and a few gulping swallows. "Ma, are you okay?"

"I just… I just never thought this day would come. I just—"

"Ma, can you talk? Dad's not there, is he?"

My father never let my mother talk on the phone for long. If she was talking to one of her girlfriends or any of her family, he'd snatch it from her hand and slam down the receiver. I've come to realize alcohol, the need to control and unjustified jealousy are an explosive combination. That was Dad from seven at night until six the next morning.

"You don't know, do you?"

"Know what?"

"Your father and I. We're separated. I've filed for divorce."

"What?" For years, it was the one thing I'd prayed for. If only she would leave him. If only he weren't around.

"I never had the strength to leave him while you kids were at home, but after Erika left, I started to see I was in danger. I didn't have the protection of being a mother. Your dad... well, there's no good way to say it. He beat me very badly one night. Other than shoves or pulling me, he'd never physically harmed me before. Just verbally and mentally attacked me while you kids were home. I called the police, but by the time they got here, he was gone. It wasn't long before they got a call about a disturbance down at Clancy's. Your dad assaulted a kid at the bar. A random kid about your age."

Why am I not surprised? I don't even know what to say.

"He's been sent to prison, Max."

"What?" I seem to have lost the power of intelligent speech. Plus, I'm swallowing tears that are sticking in my throat.

"That's when your sisters convinced me I didn't need him. He wasn't a very good provider, anyway." She sobs down the line. "And I'd long since stopped loving him."

Why didn't this happen when I was younger?

"So, I left Harbor Point and lived with Colleen for a while. Now, I have an apartment with Millie Brown. You remember her? Her husband, Seamus, died two years ago."

My throat is so tight. I finally manage to squeak, "I'm glad you're safe, Ma."

"Oh, thank you, sweetheart." More sobs. "Anyway, the divorce is almost final. Your dad isn't getting out anytime soon. Max, I'm so sorry I couldn't protect you. I wanted to. I did, but I was so scared he'd kill me or one of you. Staying with him cost me my son. Please forgive me."

"He's not my dad," I reply flatly.

Confusion in my mother's voice, she rebuts, "Yes, he is, Max."

"Biologically he is, but Mom, you're my only parent. I more than forgive you. I'm sorry I left you there to deal with him. I just had to get out."

"I know, sweet boy." She continues to heave sobs.

"Mom, I have to ask you something."

"Yes, what is it?"

"Can you forgive me for leaving?"

"There's nothing to forgive."

I heave an audible sign of relief and smile through my tears.

"Ma, I-I know this is a lot to ask, but do you think you could help me out with something?

"Anything, darling."

I tell Mom all about my life since I left—even

201

my player ways and days. I tell her all about Gallant and the strange, backward way I fell in love with Fleur.

Mom agrees to help me. Now, to convince my sisters. It shouldn't take much.

La Sylphide opens in a week. I have a lot to do before then. I'm going to need Mariette's help and maybe help from Jerome and Kandis, too.

Chapter 25

Waiting Game

Now that I have my mother and sisters back and don't have to worry about the man who fathered me, I talk to Mom and the girls every day. The only time I make the calls are during rehearsals when I'm not needed or when I go into the studio early. They're going to help me with my plan to win Fleur. Jerome is flying them in and Mariette is putting them up. And Fleur? She doesn't have a clue. She's too busy rehearsing.

One night, I stayed late at the studio to talk to Mom. Fleur went home to shower and sleep—or so I thought.

When I open the door to my apartment, there's my girl lying on my couch with her hair tumbling down her shoulders, watching *Pretty In Pink* and wearing my shirt. An unexpected, but not unwanted, surprise.

"Hi, you're here."

Fleur stands and naturally places her feet in

open fourth after unwittingly stepping her front foot through a low *passé développé*. Ballerina through and through. Graceful through and through.

I point up and down her body. "Is that my one and only dress shirt?"

"Uh-huh." She glides toward me while unbuttoning the shirt. "I can give it back."

"Keep it. I never made it look that good."

She stops in front of me, shirt completely unbuttoned. I reach up and finger the collar, sliding it between my thumb and forefinger and taking extra care not to touch her skin. Even though I'm dying to.

"Riiiight! I don't think so. Seeing you in this dress shirt that first time pushed me over the edge. It was all I could do not to jump you right in front of my grandparents. You looked good, and you knew it."

I run my finger across to her exposed collarbone and down her bare skin where the shirt is opened. "Not this good."

Fleur backs up slowly. I don't want my hands to lose touch with her cool, ivory skin, so I follow. She does a casual half pirouette and pushes me down to sit on the couch. Choreography I wish I'd thought of.

As she stands in front of me, I slide my hands from her kneecaps all the way up her hips, taking note of the lack of panties. I stand quickly and sweep the dress shirt off her shoulders.

Fleur is naked and staring at the floor.

"Eyes up, Miss Awkward."

She brings her eyes to mine. "Max, I actually love it when you give me direction. Did you know that?"

Fleur circles me slowly, peeling away the flannel shirt I'm wearing, and then with her front to my back, pulls my wifebeater over my head. She slips her small hands around my waist and down the front of my sweatpants. I gasp when she takes me in hand.

"No. I'll have to do it more often."

Oh God, her small hands working my dick have me groaning. I grow harder and harder with each stroke. I pitch my head back and rest it on her shoulder.

She drags a warm, wet kiss across my jawline. "More when we're alone than in the studio or rehearsal."

"I'll keep that in mind."

Fleur hums in my ear, and in the deepest, darkest of tones, she says, "Now, it's my turn. Take your pants off and sit on the couch."

"As you wish." I comply in seconds.

Fleur drops to her knees in front of me. She skates her hands up my thighs so delicately I can't make out if it just tickles or invigorates every cell. My dick springs into action, vibrating with want. Definitely invigorated. I lean back on the couch, and she winks before she drops her head. Fleur's silky mane brushes along my sensitive skin and I reach down to run my fingers through it. She sucks me off, root to tip. Nothing could feel better than this. Well, nothing better than being inside her. I'd love to reciprocate and taste her delicious pussy, but I'll never last that long.

"Fleur, baby."

"Mmhmm," she mumbles with me still in her mouth.

"Fleur, I'm gonna explode. I…" I pull her face away from my crotch and up to look her dead in the eye.

She gives me a mischievous smile. "Explode, huh?"

"I want you in my bed, now."

"Excellent direction, Mr. Devereaux. Lead the way."

I sit up, take her by the shoulders and help her up. She takes my hands and does the same. We *promenade à deux* into my bedroom.

Once we reach the bed, I throw off the duvet and usher her closer.

She refuses to get in. "No, you first."

"As you wish." I climb in and prop myself against the pillows.

Fleur climbs on, straddles me and then covers my chest, neck and finally my mouth with hot kisses. I try to maneuver her pelvis lower, but she shifts quickly, turns her back to me and mounts my raging hard-on with her warmth in reverse cowgirl. She places her hands on my thighs, takes hold and rides me at a trot, then canter and finally full gallop. The faster she pumps, the louder her moans. I'm about to unload at any minute, but I tell myself, *not before her*. I sit up abruptly with her stilling charging ahead, reach around and find her clit. I finger her in circles while thrusting to meet her every move.

"Oh, oh, oh, yes, yes! Omigod, yes! Aaaahhh!"

I love the crazy babble she says like she's possessed when she comes.

I follow her. "Jesus, Fleur. Oh! Omigod! Uuuuh!"

Our mutual release is followed by Fleur experiencing several orgasmic aftershocks that make her purr.

———————

Fleur is curled up under my arm, her hand on my stomach right above the happiest cock on the planet.

"Max, you seem so happy."

I chuckle. Happy? I'm blessed. "I am. I have you in my life. And my bed." I say with a flourish of my hand. "You're debuting in two weeks. There's only one thing that could make me happier."

She nuzzles the side of my chest. "I know, but I think it's important to wait. Your family—I want to know them, too."

"Yeah, I know." I smile to myself. What she doesn't know is the progress I've made and what I have up my sleeve for her.

Chapter 26

Opening Night

The ballroom at the Chicago Cultural Center with its gilded architecture and Tiffany domed skylight is the perfect venue for *La Sylphide*. It's as close to performing at the Royal Danish Theater where the ballet premiered as one can find in Chicago.

Gallant Ballet's performance of *La Sylphide* is sublime. I'm completely biased, of course, but to me, Fleur is perfect. She skips and flits and pulls off pirouettes and *jetés* that looked as if she were floating feet above the dance floor. The teeny tiny wings positioned on her costume at her lower back appear to be beating and keeping her aloft. *La Sylphide* is not a ballet that ends with a happily ever after. No, it's an extremely romantic tragedy. And yet the audience leaves with smiles on their faces, if not an ache in their hearts.

Fleur's dressing room is filled with so many well-wishers that I wait until it's cleared and she's changed to go in.

She's fully dressed in the most beautiful one-shouldered gray over pink chiffon cocktail dress and, yes, her black and white Converse. Although this pair looks new. I have to admit that high-tops look less clunky on her lovely feet, especially with the black one in a side tendu. I find her looking at the plethora of opening night flowers and notes, touching each one and sighing as she admires them.

When she looks up in the mirror and catches me watching her, I say, "You are gorgeous. Your performance was…"

"Was it?" she asks with sincerity.

She knows I was going to say "beautiful" because she pretty much knows my every thought. Which is why it has been so difficult to keep my family and the fact I flew them in for tonight a secret. I've hated lying to her, but getting my mother and sisters into town without her knowing has been a major feat. I pray the night ends the way I've planned it.

"Yes, you were amazing. Now, let's go to the after party and wait for the reviews."

"I like the first part of that idea, the second not so much. Terrifying."

"You have nothing to worry about."

———

We walk hand in hand the four minutes from the Cultural Center to Cindy's Rooftop Bar where the cast party is being held. It's September; the nights are getting colder and there's a breeze off Lake Michigan. I take off my tux jacket and place it over Fleur's exposed shoulders.

We must be some of the last to make an appearance because the rooftop bursts into applause when Fleur enters. Her grandparents rush over and deliver a multitude of hugs, kisses and effusive congratulations. Mariette stands off to the side, and when Kandis and Jerome let loose of us, she approaches slowly.

"Max, what can I say? Excellent staging. You did the original choreographer proud."

"And my Fleur-de-Lis." Mariette wraps Fleur in her arms before stepping back to finish her thought. "You were magnificent. Ethereal. I say this as a mother and the artistic director, 'Thank you for becoming part of the Gallant Ballet family. Officially.' "

Fleur takes both of Mariette's hands and squeezes them. From behind her I wrap my arms around her waist.

"Thank you, Mom. For my life and my passion for dancing." She turns her face up to catch a glimpse of my ridiculous smiling face. "And for Max."

Mariette moves close to us and whispers in Fleur's ear so I can hear. "Oh, I didn't give you

Max. You found each other. I just gave a few nudges. Badly planned nudges, but it all worked out." Mariette kisses us both on the cheeks and moves on to greet some patrons across the room.

Mariette's whisper reminds me of when we went to find Fleur in the Hamptons. Mariette whispered something in her ear then, too.

I've wondered what it was ever since, but never asked. "I want to know something, Fleur."

"What?"

"Remember when we were in the Hamptons before Mariette left us alone and we told each other we loved one another?"

"Yes, how could I forget? That was one of the worst and best nights of my life."

"Mariette whispered something to you before she left."

"She did?" Fleur's tone tells me she's playing dumb.

"You know she did. What did Mariette say to you?"

Fleur pulls me from the crowd to the edge of the roof and cuddles into my chest.

"She said, 'Fleur, make an honest man of him.' "

I pull back slightly and raise an eyebrow at her. "I'd like to be an honest man. Do you think you can do that, Fleur?" This is my opportunity to ask her to marry me.

"Max! Please. I don't want to turn you down

again. Don't ask me now. I want to meet your family first."

I wave across the room, and Fleur's gaze follows my gesture.

"Okay!"

"What do you mean, 'Okay,' Max?"

"I want you to meet my family."

My mother and sisters appear at our side just as I say the words.

I take Fleur by the shoulders and turn her to face the five most important people, other than her, in my life.

"Victoria Awkward, I'd like you to meet my mother, Maeve Delaney, and my sisters—Janine, Colleen, Abby and Erika."

Fleur claps several times, disbelief on her face. "Your family? They're here?"

"Everyone but my father. I don't think you'll get to meet him. I'll tell you about it later. In the meantime, Mom, girls, this is my girlfriend, Victoria Awkward. Fleur." Wow! That's the first time I've said *girlfriend* aloud.

Fleur offers her hand, but my mother flies at her and engulfs her in a big Irish hug. My sisters follow suit.

They shower her with words of gratitude.

"Thank you for giving me my boy back."

"We have a brother again. Thank you."

Fleur's head pops out of the scrum of estrogen. "Max, When? How?"

213

"I've been talking to them for a while. Planning the trip here. Mariette and your grandparents have been helping me."

Fleur excuses herself repeatedly and squirms away from my family's embrace. She makes her way back to me. My mother and sisters look confused.

Fleur squares her shoulders and says loud enough for everyone on the roof and perhaps some down on Michigan Avenue to hear, "Ask me now, Max. Ask me right now."

"Right here in front of everyone?"

"Yes, please."

"As you wish." I drop to one knee for the third time and take Fleur's left hand.

"Miss Victoria Awkward, I was shell of a man. I was self-involved, lonely and frankly, a jerk. I took, but never gave, and for that I will always be sorry. Then you came to Gallant and into my world with your terrible—sorry, Jer and Kandis—last name, your weird shoe thing and that ancient motorcycle, and I was intrigued. I saw you dance, and I was bewitched. I got to know your heart, and I was a goner. I love everything about you. Mostly, I love how you love me, flawed as I am. I love that you encouraged me to give my family another chance. I missed them more than I allowed myself to admit, and you knew it, even when I didn't. I've been looking for my true home for so long, and I've found it with you."

214

There's a lot of sniffling and watery eyes in the room. Mostly the ballerinas and Mom and my sisters and Mariette, but Jerome scrubs at his eyes with his thumbs and index fingers.

"Please give me the chance to love you forever. You can keep the name Ward or Awkward. Whatever you want. I don't care about that anymore. It's hard to believe it was so important. And now, for the third time... Fleur, will you marry me and make an honest man of me.
"

Fleur pitches herself at me, throwing her arms around my neck with grace, as only a ballerina can do, and I catch her.

She says loud enough that it echoes, "Yes, of course, yes. What took you so long?"

The entire company and our mutual families break into riotous laughter.

Then I kiss her, gently, reverently and whisper in her ear, "Thanks a million."

———

By the time *Desperately Seeking Susan* premieres in May, she's Victoria Ward-Devereaux.

But those of us who love her?

We call her Fleur.

215

Epilogue

The Reviews Are In for *La Sylphide*:

"As the sylph, the slight, but mighty Victoria Ward instilled the role with a swift delicacy, which informed her role as the object of James, the hero's, desire and downfall. Her eventual bittersweet death is so romantic it is worthy of an ugly cry by even the most staid of balletgoers."

Chicago River Times

"Ballet has a new star with a vintage pedigree. Victoria Ward, the daughter of the recently revealed partners in dance and 'real life,' Mariette Gallant and Jerome Ward, made her debut in *La Sylphide* tonight. She has inherited her mother's poise and her father's power to move. Brava to Miss Ward and Bravissimo to Gallant Ballet."

En Pointe Magazine

"Watch out, Peter Madsen! Gallant Ballet with their new talent, Victoria Ward, and the staging of their choreographer, Max Devereaux, is a force to be reckoned with."

New York Tribune

"Gallant Ballet's *La Sylphide* is a heartrending romp through love, betrayal, loss and redemption. Miss Victoria Ward as the sylph bounded into the audience's heart from her first series of turns across the floor...."

Dance Universe

Acknowledgements

Thank you:

Janine Savage and Jen Matera from the Write Divas. Thank you is not enough. You're tough and thorough and make me work harder and therefore, better.

Lucy V.-my ballet consultant

Sarah Hansen from Okay Creations. Thank you for my beautiful cover. I don't know how you do it, but you always get it right.

Kristen Hope Mazzola for formatting and just being generally awesome.

My Beta readers: Brian, Marjorie, Kellie and Theresa

Anne Wathen, my legal consultant. Thanks for keeping me organized and legal.

My fellow authors/friends and book bloggers, some I've never met in person, but who have inspired and helped me even if they didn't know it.

I need to call out a few by name:
Isabelle Peterson
Liv Morris
Rachel Robinson
Theresa Troutman

Jennifer Probst

T.S. Irons

Z.B. Heller

Staci Hart

Brittainy C. Cherry

Alice Clayton

Megan Hart

And Jamie McGuire-for your FAQs for Writers page on your website. It's where I learned how to be in this business.

The talented authors of Awesome, BFFs and 101.

And last-the loves of my life, The Connor Boys: Brian, Ian, Sean and Jasper. I love you all so much.

About the Author

Emme Burton is the author of the Top 50 Rom-Com, SNACK and the Better Than Series: Better Than Me, Fix It For Us, and Still Into You. She is a contributing author to the best-selling books Hook & Ladder 69 and Bleed Blue 69. She lives in St. Louis, Missouri with her amazing husband and sons and her "fur boy." Emme has never, ever been lost in a mall either as a child or an adult. Her mother, and now her family, have always known where to find her. At the bookstore.

Like Emme's Facebook Page: Author Emme Burton

Follow her on Twitter: @EmmeBurton

Add her books to your TBR on GoodReads.

Emme's Website: www.emmeburton.com

More Books by Emme Burton:

Better Than Me (Book 1, Better Than Series)
Fix It For Us (Book 2, Better Than Series)
Still Into You (Book 3, Better Than Series)
Snack
Hook & Ladder 69, 18 Authors, 1 Hot Firehouse
(An Anthology)
Bleed Blue 69, 25 Authors, 1 Police Station
(An Anthology)

www.ingramcontent.com/pod-product-compliance
Lightning Source LLC
Chambersburg PA
CBHW032117170626
46808CB00006B/1984